T0271548

Tomorrow, Berlin

Tomorrow, Berlin

Oscar Coop-Phane

Translated from the French
by George Miller

A

Arcadia Books Ltd
139 Highlever Road
London W10 6PH

www.arcadiabooks.co.uk

First published in the United Kingdom 2015
Originally published as *Demain, Berlin* by Finitude Editions 2013

A catalogue record for this book is available from the British Library.

ISBN 978-1-910050-46-0

Typeset in Minion by MacGuru Ltd
Printed and bound by CPI Group (UK) Ltd., Croydon CR0 4YY

Arcadia Books supports English PEN *www.englishpen.org* and The Book Trade Charity *www.btbs.org*

Arcadia Books distributors are as follows:

in the UK and elsewhere in Europe:
Macmillan Distribution Ltd
Brunel Road
Houndmills
Basingstoke
Hants RG21 6XS

in the USA and Canada:
Dufour Editions
PO Box 7
Chester Springs
PA 19425

in Australia/New Zealand:
NewSouth Books
University of New South Wales
Sydney NSW 2052

PART ONE

The Removal of Pain

I

Tobias isn't very tall. He has brown hair. Sometimes his voice sounds like a madwoman's or a little boy's, as though he's never recovered from his childhood. He's capable of being extremely calm, but most of the time he flaps about like crazy, to escape his black butterflies.

He couldn't have lived without crutches. So even if the drugs are ruining him, destroying him gradually, that's preferable to dying suddenly, drowning himself in the Spree or hanged with his belt.

It's not that he doesn't have the courage to go on living, just that he's taken such a pummelling that he's no longer cut out for it. The drugs save him, in the same way that they kill other people. It's a slow destruction guided by his instinct for self-preservation. That stops him doing the deed, bringing the final, brutal blow down on his neck.

Tobias's childhood was tragic in the way that an item of local news can be. His uncle tore him apart, gave him years of pain though no one would believe him. Whenever he went to Cologne, it was always the same story, he knew his uncle would grip him in his strong arms and he'd go home a bit more damaged. But he wouldn't talk about it; nobody had believed him the first time, so he learned to keep quiet, zip his mouth. He would only be in his uncle's clutches for a week, eventually he'd return to his father; no one would take care of him, but they wouldn't do him harm. Then back he'd go to school, far away from his uncle until the next holidays. A few months' peace.

Tobias has never liked holidays.

No one really knew what to do with this child who'd already tried to kill himself by the time he was seven by sticking his head in the hand basin. He was sent off to his mother in New York, far from his father's native Germany.

That was the time when the uncle died, when they'd finally sent Tobias far away, when he was almost old enough to defend himself. Life's little ironies.

In the United States his mother was as loving as a mother can be when she comes to it late. By then, the dice had been cast; childhood had left its mark. She didn't really know what to make of this son who was gradually becoming an adult. She didn't know what to do with her affection.

Without going into it too deeply, she sensed that Tobias had already been broken. Before she went off to her job at the airport, she would always leave him some money on the kitchen table and something nice to heat up, carefully wrapped in tinfoil. She didn't know what else to do. From time to time, she took him to the cinema.

Tobias didn't talk much, as though he didn't feel the need.

Every day he would get up, go to school, speak English, carefully throw the dish his mother had made into the communal bin so that she didn't find the remains and buy a hotdog or a slice of pizza from the place on the corner with the dollars from the kitchen table.

He walked the streets, then went back home. He waited for his mother.

They'd talk a bit about his day, eat again and sleep, the best that life could offer.

He was spending his life going through the motions.

Tobias was lonely, but above all, he was bored.

He could have chosen books or music. He chose drugs. Maybe because he was given them, maybe because they better answered his needs. They offered a sense of risk, a life distinct from other people's, as though a new part of the world awaited.

He discovered unfamiliar sensations, his boredom vanished, and a warm sense of pleasure enveloped him gently and completely. He met people who were a bit like him, but somehow different. They liked this new kid, who was younger than them, a bit of a laugh, always happy to do you a favour.

Because above all, Tobias wants to please. With a fix or with food, gifts or letters.

He's not a solitary addict, for him drugs are something to share, like love. To be enjoyed together, away from the rest of the world. Tobias likes drug addicts even more than drugs. He shuts himself away with them. With their little routines, their regular life, a petit-bourgeois life at home around the mirror. Curtains closed, among friends, stay-at-homes. The old druggie girls are there, gossiping; always the same faces – far away from the non-believers. You have to avoid non-addicts like the plague.

He joined their circle and hasn't been able to leave, no matter where he lands. Always the same little circle, the closed world of people convinced they're living more intensely.

When he turned twenty, he went to live with his sister in Paris. They'd spent very little time together before. When Tobias was sent to New York, his sister, who was three years older, ended up with their grandfather in France. Families get torn apart when no one knows what to do with them.

Even though they hardly knew each other any more, there was something strong which bound them together, though it would be hard to say if it was blood or childhood memories. But he wasn't really seeking a reunion; he'd come to break free. She had no idea; she took him in without a murmur, as a brother.

Another new language, new streets to wander. Tobias grew up rootless. He felt more American than German. Soon perhaps France would suit him.

They lived in a small apartment on the rue Campagne-Première. Tobias slept on the couch, which has long been his habit. Every day his sister went off to work. Tobias didn't really understand what she did; on the phone, she talked about client meetings and interests to safeguard. But in the evening, he waited for her, as he had done with his mother all those years.

They led a quiet life. During the day, Tobias

explored the new city. He was learning French, walking the streets. Then, with nothing better to do, he made dinner. At the weekend, they went to the cinema.

Tobias thought about drugs. This clean life was a bit dull. He didn't mention it. His sister was well aware that there was something in him that was damaged, but she didn't dwell on it.

She met Stéphane; he was a colleague; it was an office romance. It soon became awkward for Tobias, the gooseberry brother. They got tired of going out as a threesome, of the depressive younger brother sleeping on the sofa, the nice kid who, apart from the meals he made, didn't seem to be doing much to tackle the emptiness of his life.

Tobias's idleness got on Stéphane's nerves. For God's sake, he was a man now, he needed to work, find an apartment. You can't stay on your sister's sofa all your life; you can't make soup like a kept woman. Come on, old son, show a bit of spunk. You have to grapple with life, climb the ladder. There'll be time for sitting by the fireside later, but first there's the race. You need to sweat, get out of breath, sweat some more. You know Paris now, you know how it works. Find a job. Flex your muscles. You'll get eaten alive otherwise. If you don't fight, that's what happens. You're just a juicy bit of prey lying quietly on the sofa. I know people, we'll find you a job. But if you're not up for it, there's nothing I can do. It's a war, mate. It's a war, and if you don't run, you get shot at. Avoid the traps, jump into the holes and crawl forward. It's not too late. You can do it. I'm saying this because I like you. And I love your sister. And you know, it's driving us apart, having you in between us. I don't want that. It's time you made your way in life. You're a man, so get on your feet. You need to run. Get breathless and sweat – breathless and sweat.

OK, let's try what you've cooked up today. You're a good lad. I like you, you know. And I love your sister.

Stéphane both attracted and repelled Tobias. He looked so strong, as if troubles just slid off him. Life's misfortunes had no purchase on Stéphane. He stood tall, a proud big guy, like a soldier with his short haircut. Tobias was the reject from the ranks. He needed crutches to limp his way through life.

And since the soldier always wins, Tobias had to get up off the sofa. He found an attic on the rue des Écoles and a job in a café on the boulevard Saint-Michel.

At first, his colleagues really took the piss out of him. He was so effeminate, like a poof. And that's exactly what he was, but he couldn't say that to them.

He didn't know what to tell them. They were men like Stéphane. Hardened against life, proud of their clothes and their bearing. And they talked about the chicks they were screwing and Tobias felt alone. He did his job and he felt bored. A small Vichy and two espressos; the bill for table eight; a white coffee and two hot chocolates; the bill for table eight, the bill for table eight.

And every day he put on his black waistcoat with all the pockets for coins, he carried his aluminium tray, he opened bottles of Ricqlès and Cacolac. He made a decent living, with his shifts and his tips, paid daily and in cash. He caught on quickly and worked hard. And his colleagues began to take to him, even if he never went for a drink after their shift.

This one time, though, he did go along. They'd had a rotten day. Nothing but guys knocking back cappuccinos with hot girls. All of them the sort who look like they never do a day's work.

At the end of their shift they went to another joint on the rue d'Assas. The owner didn't make them pay and there was a chance of picking up a chick. They had Picon beer and cocaine. So Tobias put a straw up his nose; he was with his colleagues, a long way from his New York friends, but he still did it to feel alive, to stop thinking about things, to feel as strong as Stéphane.

They got really wasted that night on the rue d'Assas.

So he'd relapsed a bit but he didn't worry. He finally had something in common with his colleagues, with Maurice, Paulo and Gégé. Like he belonged to a group and that felt really good. Life went on like that, between the attic on the rue des Écoles and the bar on the boulevard Saint-Michel, punctuated by the lines he did.

In the apartment block on the rue des Écoles, staircase C, on the top floor where you find the attics and poverty, and where everyone shits in the communal toilet, Tobias made friends with his nearest neighbour.

Jérôme didn't seem to work. He got up late and listened to music. Tobias could hear it clearly through the walls on his days off. That man had a very different life; you got the feeling he had time to have fun.

Perhaps because they were immediate neighbours, Tobias and Jérôme became friends. They'd have a drink together in one apartment or the other. For the first time in his life, Tobias found himself speaking openly – and for the first time someone listened.

One evening when they were drinking grappa, Tobias offered Jérôme some cocaine. He hesitated at first, then said something like, 'If you fancy it, I've got a pick-me-up, something we take at work.' Jérôme laughed, 'Ah, if I'd known you were into that… Go on then, give me a line and the next one's on me.' He had a good laugh; cocaine was his bread and butter.

They did coke all evening and danced a bit to the music from Jérôme's turntable. They talked quickly, as though there was an urgent need to unload all the thoughts that came whizzing into their heads.

Grappa evenings became coke evenings, in one apartment or the other, talking, as before.

Paulo and Maurice's gear was rubbish compared to Jérôme's. One day, Tobias let them try some at work. No contest, this was the real deal. You couldn't feel your teeth, your mind buzzed with ideas, you stopped feeling sick of life.

Tobias and Jérôme went into partnership. In the bar on the boulevard alone there were plenty of takers.

For Jérôme, all this was temporary. He wanted to leave his attic far behind and go to Montevideo to be with the only woman he'd ever loved. He talked about it all the time. This life would soon be a thing of the past; then it would be sunshine and Luisa, the little business they'd set up together, the taste of freedom in his mouth. But he needed to buy his plane ticket and have some money for when he got there; he couldn't very well arrive with nothing in his pocket.

He'd met Luisa just a week before she returned to her country. But he knew instantly that she was the woman he'd marry.

There was no Luisa for Tobias, but it was nice making a bit of money – perhaps one day he'd be able to move out.

Business was easy. Jérôme looked after the supply – he had contacts – and the regulars, the people he'd known for ages. Tobias supplied the café on the boulevard, but only his colleagues or customers he knew – he mustn't get nabbed.

And it turned out that between them they knew a lot of people. The money rolled in. The work wasn't unpleasant, a few handshakes and as many drugs as you wanted, a seemingly endless supply. Tobias worked less at the café on the boulevard. From time to time he saw his sister.

She was going to marry Stéphane. They wanted children.

Then, since Tobias didn't have a Luisa, Jérôme decided to find him one. He'd been by himself long enough.

Tobias found it hard explaining to Jérôme that he liked boys, that it was a Louis that he needed. But that was no problem for Jérôme. He liked both girls and boys himself.

So he took Tobias to gay bars. A new world opened up, a world of easy, rough sex; of getting high and sweaty bodies; of hands touching him, grasping him all over his body; of stiff cocks and strong arms.

They sold a bit of cocaine there, but mainly they fucked until they could take no more; cocks and arses until they were sick of them.

It calmed Tobias down. Whenever he got bored, he would slip into those bars; people recognised him, he was part of that world. It felt like a secret, the sense of belonging to a scene and especially the anger he got out of his system among those stripped bodies, all keyed up to satisfy his desires – yes, all of it, the atmosphere, the emotion and the anger gave him a kind of wisdom, the wisdom of a calm man. It was in these stinking bars, soaked in violence, sweat, brutality and passion, that Tobias discovered that other people could give him pleasure, that drugs were not the only thing that could make his soul quiver. Other people, other bodies could also be part of it, could serve his pleasure.

He began to like his life. He had a strange feeling, like when you return from a journey – a feeling of having changed, of wanting to describe everything but finding the words won't come, other people wouldn't understand. He felt he had something to live for. It didn't really matter that it was sex and drugs; he'd found a place, somewhere he could come to rest. He felt legitimate among other people. Yes, he had found the right place to come to rest, no one would tell him off. It was an incredible feeling to know he'd found his place. He's there, being touched – not with the fingertips, but the whole hand, because he belongs.

The days flew by, in the orgy bars, at the café on the boulevard, in his attic. He grabbed cocks, he carried his tray, he made up little bags of cocaine. He liked being alone with his digital scales. A decent heap on his left, a knife and pieces of plastic. You make a gram, always a little bit less – business is business. You seal the plastic with your lighter. And that little ball instantly represents money. You do the calculations, you're safe.

You have lots of little balls sealed in plastic, you'll put them in your pocket and sell them. That's the raw material.

It felt really good being able to pay the rent without worrying, drink whatever he wanted, buy cigarettes without counting his change.

Soon he only worked weekends in the café on the boulevard. Fridays and Saturdays were when there were most customers for the little balls in plastic bags. At the end of his shift, he'd tour the rue d'Assas with Maurice, Paulo and Gégé. He did a line or two with them and there were more clients there, so that was extra money rolling in – like Molloy with his pebbles, he stuck the notes in his left pocket and took out a ball sealed in plastic from his right – an endless cycle. He also felt he was giving them pleasure; he was selling a bit of happiness. Didn't he also take some of that happiness himself whenever he wanted? He had that in common with them, the little artificial excitement, the awakening of the soul. Oh, how he would have loved to be like that all the time, without having to stick a straw up his nose.

One Monday night, he met Victor in one of the orgy bars. They fucked like crazy. The difference was, with Victor he felt satisfied. He didn't feel the need to go and look for other arses, to be penetrated by other cocks. He felt full of Victor. That was enough for him. Their bodies completed each other as though they could talk to each other, as if this case went beyond them.

Victor was thirty-five, about ten years older than Tobias. They exchanged names. Tobias didn't have a phone; he jotted down Victor's number.

They kissed shyly as they parted outside the bar where they met, as though they wanted to recreate the embarrassment of a less brutal encounter, as though they had not already fucked in that filthy bar, rammed with bodies.

'Will you call me?'

'Yes. You'll need to wait a bit.'

Day was breaking. It was cold, but in a nice way. Tobias smoked as he walked slowly along – he was enraptured. If you'd looked closely at his face as he walked home after that strange night, you'd have seen a little smile on his lips. Not the smile of a drunk, but something suggesting happiness was within reach. You can sense it, it's there; you could almost touch it, the happiness of enchantment.

He could sense the little nostalgic smile crease his cheeks; he felt like he was observing himself walking in the streets, a figure alone, but already as though he was missing Victor.

It was almost seven when Tobias reached the rue des Écoles. All the way there, his little smile had remained. It disappeared instantly when he saw Jérôme outside the building being led to a police van in handcuffs.

Their eyes met. Jérôme motioned to him to get away. There was no sense in him getting picked up too. They'd both go down, and what good was that?

Tobias obeyed. He passed the building one last time and kept walking. He just kept going.

II

Armand's a nice guy. Whether people like him or not, that's generally what they think; a nice loser, with tangled hair and jeans that are too short. He mooches round the bars hoping to catch the eye of some hot girl. Armand says he wants to be a painter; he works at it a bit every morning. On the street he looks for pieces of wood and road signs. He likes having paint splashes on his hands, arms or legs as proof of what he's doing. He also likes the idea that he's working with something physical, one foot in reality, the other in creativity. It's the physical sense of the moment when he's painting that he likes; otherwise, maybe he'd have wanted to write.

He plays the drum machine. He doesn't eat much. He smokes plenty, though. It's unusual to run into Armand without a cigarette end dangling from his lips. It doesn't go with his look, the extinguished butt he chews at the corner of his mouth. Armand's young and quite good-looking. He has four scooters; one day, he's going to buy a motorbike. And then he'll finally be free; he'll ride around in the desert, a law unto himself, the stars and stripes tattooed on his shoulder.

At sixteen he left his mother's house to live with a girl he loved more than life itself, as he put it. He truly believed that.

She'd sent him emails without him knowing who she was. He saw a girl in the high school yard and hoped it was her.

The emails were funny; every evening he had to reply, find something new to say. God, this girl wasn't like the rest; she was definitely right for him. He was afraid. There was also the tall blonde he looked at outside the school smoking her morning Dunhill.

If only the email girl and the Dunhill blonde could be the same. But surely she couldn't be, that would be too beautiful, and life's not beautiful; in this life you stumble and fall, land on your arse.

In their emails, they talked about meeting. He knew she went to his school and that she was a year older than him, but there were so many girls in the final year.

Then it was arranged; they'd meet at the crappy party organised by the student committee in a nightclub on the place de la Madeleine. Armand would be DJing and playing his drum machine. She'd come and speak to him; at least she knew who he was.

Armand was a bit drunk when he arrived at the party. The tall blonde was there, on her phone outside. But it couldn't be her – there were dozens of girls in their final year. Well, time would tell.

Armand went into the nightclub. He felt proud of his big bag of records. He focused on this prop to forget his fear of meeting the girl who'd been writing to him.

He said hello to good friends, then went up to the cabin where they played the records. There was a small spiral staircase up to the little cabin with two turntables and a view of the dance floor. He could see the tops of all his friends' heads;

he'd set the drum machine going and get them dancing.

He played his favourite records. It seemed to be going well; from up in his little cabin, he could see heads and arms moving mechanically. Two girls came up the spiral staircase; they slipped him a note without him seeing their faces.

My first rhymes with 'you'. My second I drink each morning. My third is a dog. The whole thing is attached to the bottom of my face.

He felt a pang holding this little scrap of paper. At last, he could see her writing, her real writing, letters shaped by her hand, not the impersonal characters on the computer. He didn't understand the riddle at first; what could she have stuck to the bottom of her face?

But of course – a beauty spot! Bew – Tea – Spot!

Did the blonde have a beauty spot on her chin? He didn't know, he'd only seen her from a distance. He had to stop thinking about the Dunhill blonde. If letter-girl was someone else, he'd take her anyway, he needed a chick.

When he'd finished playing his records, he went down on to the dance floor. People spoke to him; he even got some compliments. He didn't hear them; he was smoking and looking for the beauty spot.

Finally she came up to him, the pretty blonde. They shook hands. They agreed on a café for the following day. Then she left without looking back.

That evening Armand felt happy as he fell asleep. It was her, and tomorrow they'd have coffee.

In the café they talked about Matthew Barney and anarchy. Armand managed to pronounce the word 'anthropomorphism'. He was proud of that. Later, Emma told him that had impressed her.

They smoked a lot, Cravens for him, Dunhills for her; they had three coffees each. They were a bit awkward, but kept the conversation going; there was a sort of urgency to express what they wanted to say.

For a month they met like this in the café, without getting closer in any other way, the way of love. It was understood though that it would happen, that it was inevitable they'd kiss.

Armand was afraid. Emma reckoned it wasn't up to her to make the first move. What would happen after, when they were ready to make love? The whole deal of being a couple scared Armand, yet it was what he wanted most.

One day, like many times before, they parted in the metro, in the corridors of Montparnasse station; she went towards line 9 and the little apartment in La Muette (a half-forgiven mistake: 'Do I really look like I live in La Muette?') where she lived alone on the floor above her grandmother – and he towards line 12, to his mother's three-room apartment on the rue de la Convention. Again without kissing, they each went their separate ways, towards that dull life in which they were no longer together.

Armand was hungry. He wanted to buy some sweets from the vending machine on the platform of line 12. He accidentally pressed the wrong button and some madeleines came out. Armand didn't want to admit defeat. He took out another coin; he got the right button. While he was doing this, the train went by. He'd catch the next one; he wanted sweets.

He leaned against one of those high seats designed to stop tramps sleeping on them. He was eating his sweets and waiting for the next train. Emma appeared on the platform right in front of him looking flustered. Without giving him time to take this in, she kissed him. A first kiss that tasted of jellies.

III

Franz has the same name as his father. Franz Riepler. Exactly the same. This is not a very good omen. The father died young, newly wed, in a hunting accident. A stray bullet. One minute he was standing there, the next he was down. The child his wife was carrying still unborn. Guts ruptured, aware he was dying, on his knees on a carpet of brown leaves in the beautiful Bavarian forest. Our son will live, but you won't be there to see him, but they'll give him your name so that he knows you would have treasured him, if the bullet had struck elsewhere.

The mother is sad. She brings Franz up as all she has left. See how like his father he is. His smile, the look in his eye. He's not called Franz Riepler for nothing. He has the same way of frowning.

That's how little Franz grew up, like a photograph that keeps changing, the piece of photographic paper his mother treasured; sadly, the living image of what fate had snatched from her.

He and his mother left Bavaria, since there was nothing for them to do there, since there was no more father working at the sawmill. Mother and child, on their own, making a life for themselves. Dinah, the mother, found a job as a chambermaid in the home of an industrialist in Lübeck. Franz, the child, went too. He was four. A long journey, then arriving on a cold, grey day in the big middle-class house of the Kienzel family, manufacturers of wine-bottle corks.

It was quite something, the big house built of brick, the park that extended as far as the eye could see, a pond, outbuildings. This would be a good place for Franz to grow up. They were an influential family, a fine family. The children ran around in the garden. Soon, Franz would join in their play, pulling Katherine's hair, fighting with Georg like they were brothers, since they were growing up together. The mother performed thankless tasks, humiliating chores, the sort where you wipe away other people's filth. Ironing Sir's shirts, brushing Madam's wigs, scrubbing Sir's shit off the toilet, throwing away Madam's tampons. Rebuffing the caretaker's advances, doing the shopping. Anyhow, Franz grew up with them, he learned their manners, he pulled little Katherine's hair, he fought with Georg, like they were brothers.

Soon Franz turned fifteen. He fell in love with Katherine. She had such soft skin, such long hair.

They had to hide it: brother and sister can't fall in love; nor can you love the maid's son.

It was bliss. At night Franz would get into Katherine's bed. They made love simply, as two young people do. They felt they were experiencing something unique, something that other people could never know. The touching belief of young lovers, cut off from the rest of the world since they live for what others – so they think – could never feel.

Franz would go to Katherine at midnight. He'd sleep in her bed, and at around 5 a.m., before the household awoke, he'd creep back upstairs alone to wait for morning.

During the day, he stayed in his room, so as not to see Katherine, to avoid his feelings for her bursting out in front of everyone and betraying their love.

He had to keep busy. He took books from Sir's library. Finally, among those yellowed pages and austere bindings, he could be himself.

Franz's asceticism pleased Sir. The maid's son might make something of himself after all; he wanted to be progressive enough to think so.

Dinah fell ill. Bronchitis, with serious complications, mucus in the lungs. Trussed up in bed, the ceiling of her little room looked like her destination in the sky.

Dinah died. No more mother and child. Just

Franz, and the Kienzel family, who had no idea what to do with him.

Sir and Madam discussed it. Katherine prayed about her anxieties. Franz had to stay; he had to sleep in her arms again. He could replace the caretaker. He could live in the little shed; she could be with him at night, as before.

She spoke to her father. No, we have Jules, I can't sack him. But you know very well that Jules is useless. Yes, my dear, I know. And Franz is crafty, I know that too. That boy spends his days reading. Maybe he'll be a poet, who knows? His mother was a good woman, I must do all I can for her son. I shall send him to school. I'll pay. The boy will make something of himself, we'll give him all the help we can. Why are you crying, my dear? I thought you liked the boy, you grew up together. I want to give him the best. Why are you crying?

In Hannover there is a boarding school they call the Institute. There boys – boys from good families – are taught philosophy, literature, geography, mathematics and history. Six hours of lessons a day, sport, and a uniform in the British style. Franz liked it there. He sent long letters to Katherine, the kind of letters you keep, which pile up in a nice metal tin. Later, though we may not read them any more, we take them with us when we move house, we can't throw them away because they are evidence of what we once were.

When the weekend came, the other boys went home to their families. Franz stayed behind because he no longer had any family. He remained in his little cell. He studied, and wrote too, some touching, well-wrought verses about the seasons, nature, and also death. Love he reserved for Katherine. Her skin was so soft, her hair so long.

He made friends. Jojo the Legend, Günther and Barnabé. They smoked in secret behind the observatory. It didn't go very far, just some short-lived, cautious silliness. In a few months, they would get their diplomas, so best not get caught. Anyway, what would Sir think if he discovered that thanks to his money Franz was smoking with Jojo the Legend behind the observatory?

Franz studied hard. He also learned nice manners. He was a fervent admirer of Aristotle. A little bust of the philosopher with a full beard was positioned above his bed. Maybe Franz's essays were confused and disorganised, but so inspired, so sincere that his results turned out to be entirely acceptable. He was a bit of a dabbler, true, but it was enlightened dilettantism, to the delight of his teachers, who saw in him – they saw this so rarely – a student who was passionate about their subject.

The results arrived. Franz was second in his class. He was seventeen now. No more Institute, but the life of men, on his own, with his diploma in his pocket.

He hitched back to Lübeck along desolate industrial roads lined with factories and power stations. All those buildings, all this activity spurred him on. He too would be such a man: he would build things. For heaven's sake, he'd come second in his class at the Institute in Hannover!

He knocked on the Kienzels' door, unexpectedly, without warning them he was coming, since it was his childhood home, since Katherine was there. She was beautiful, she was gentle, he loved her. Of course, over time, they hadn't written to each other so much, but throughout those two years, Franz had not stopped thinking about her. Their love could be out in the open now; there was no shame any more. Franz was no longer the maid's son, he had his diploma, he'd come second at the Institute in Hannover; he was wearing his uniform like a blazon over his heart.

A grey, unsmiling woman opened the door.

'How may I help, sir?'

'I'm Franz.'

'Franz? We're not expecting any Franz. What do you want? Are you here for the wedding?'

'What wedding? No, I've come to see the Kienzels.'

'Come in for a moment, please. I'll call Madam.'

Madam appeared.

'Franz! How handsome you are. And that uniform! You're a man now.'

'You're very elegant too, madam.'

'You've come for Katherine's wedding. That's lovely. I'll have a room made up for you. We'll get you a suit too. Tomorrow will be a day of celebration. Come along with me. My husband will be so pleased to see you. Ah, who would have thought that you'd turn out so handsome! It's wonderful, Franz, you're a man!'

With Sir, he talked about the Institute, his diploma, Aristotle, plans for a career. But where could Katherine be? Was she really getting married? Yes, she was. How could she no longer love him?

The conversation with Sir dragged on. He had contacts, in Munich, Berlin, Hannover. Franz could take his pick. They would find him a job.

But where was Katherine? That was all Franz could think about.

He found himself alone in a room that wasn't his. He still hadn't seen Katherine. He tried on the suit that he would wear in honour of her love, in honour of her love for someone else. Hadn't she read his letters? God, he loved her, he'd told her so. All those nights they'd spent together! It wasn't possible that she loved someone else. He felt something in his gut; a growing sense of injustice within him, crushing his entrails, then his ribcage. It welled up in his gorge. He threw up all the tears in his body. But the bad feeling was still there. The melancholy bile seemed to keep on coming endlessly. Throwing up or yelling would do no good. This bad feeling would always be there. He wanted to write about it, but he couldn't. Soon it would be time for dinner; he would see Katherine.

The groom was as expected. Short, rather dim. No light in his eyes; no refinement in his features. So that's the sort of man she likes, Franz thought. Rather empty, kind, with a job, comfortably off. He, a maid's son, could not compete on that terrain, even if he did come second at the Institute.

Then Katherine appeared. Something in her eyes had changed. She looked nice, her hair shone as before, but she had lost her distinctive beauty. Katherine loved a little fool; she was no longer what she had been, there was no nobility in her features. She had found her place, in the bed of the petty bourgeoisie. And now Franz wanted nothing to do with that place for anything in the world; he was alone.

At dinner they talked about the financial crisis and safeguarding interests. The changing world, all that stuff, property prices and petrochemicals. The industrialists' equivalent of peasants discussing the weather.

Katherine tried to catch Franz's eye as if to seek forgiveness. But she couldn't, he'd already moved on.

IV

Tobias walked on for a short time, dazed by what he'd just experienced. Day was breaking. He needed somewhere to sleep. Going to his sister's was out of the question – imagine Stéphane's face if he showed up there! That left Victor. He could ask him that much, after all.

Tobias was cold; he kept walking. He needed to find a phone box, and hope Victor was at home and would pick up. The boulevard Saint-Germain was deserted, a few workers, like well-dressed tramps emerging from a hard night, and Tobias, alone again, searching for a telephone, searching for a bed.

He went into a café. He was struck by the noise of the coffee machine, beans being ground, milk heated. At the counter there were just men on their own, lost amid the mechanical noise, like workers who have left machines running while they come to. No conversation, no music, just the incessant noise of the coffee machine for all these lonely men up at this hour.

On one side, the owner was reading a newspaper and across the counter, the men, regularly spaced, stood staring into their own private void, the void of their early morning existence. From time to time, one of them put a coin down on the counter, breaking the silence: 'Have a good day.' Heads would look up, and the man would leave, as though he'd never been. Men came and went – and always the incessant noise, the metallic noise of the coffee machine.

The owner got up from his paper – he looked at Tobias as though he hadn't expected anything from him.

'Have you got a phone?'

The owner glanced at the other side of the bar. 'Over there.' Tobias saw the phone.

He took some coins from his pocket and unfolded the scrap of paper with Victor's number on it. The men at the bar were watching. The owner was reading his paper again.

'Victor? It's me… I hoped you'd pick up. I was scared you wouldn't… I need you, Victor. Where do you live? Great, I'm on my way.'

In the metro from the gare du Nord, Tobias tried to think about Jérôme, but he couldn't; all that mattered was finding a bed, finally lying down and sleeping, and never waking up.

Victor didn't ask questions. He and Tobias fell asleep, nestled together.

Tobias lived with Victor on the rue de Dunkerque. They shared a bed and everything else: showers, casseroles, clothes.

Victor worked in PR. The apartment was comfortable. Tobias was too scared to go back to the café on the boulevard Saint-Michel. The thought of the rue des Écoles, the whole of the Left Bank, messed with his head a bit. He couldn't go near it. The Left Bank meant the police and prison, communal showers and beatings.

But before long he had to make up his mind to go and look for what he rather childishly referred to as his 'jackpot'. That would keep him afloat for a while, but only if he went back, up the staircase on the rue des Écoles, past Mrs Gérard's door.

He went at night; even cops had to sleep. Everything was normal, the entry code hadn't changed, the stairwell still smelled of fried food and the cellar. The packet was there too, where he'd left it, wrapped up and hidden in the gas pipes. Tobias slipped it into his jacket and ran off as though escaping that whole part of his life.

Yet he often thought about his garret, about Paulo, Maurice and Gégé on the boulevard, and especially about Jérôme and the morning he got picked up; the poor guy, he'll never be with Luisa, but he'll keep writing to her, dreaming of Montevideo from behind bars in a small, filthy cell.

It should have been him: Tobias was the one who should have got caught; he didn't have a Luisa.

Oh, but he did now, things had changed, he had Victor and all those days spent waiting for him. He was befuddled by his love, unable to think of anything else. Evenings brought relief; he would go and meet Victor outside his grey office, they'd have hot chocolate and hold each other tight in a male embrace, separate from other people, as though nothing could happen to them. Now he was with Victor, Tobias was saved, the end of his wandering made sense.

Of course in time there were arguments, violent ones more often than not, men's fights; they'd both get high, too, before or after fucking, as if their unity as a couple needed this little additional thrill. They lived attached to one another, one inside the other.

The jackpot was almost used up. Tobias got a job in a local bar; it was the only work he knew, after all. But it was a far cry from the café on the boulevard Saint-Michel. In this place there was no uniform, no black waistcoat or white shirt; it had what the boss called 'a relaxed feel'. No professional baristas; the people he worked with had had quite strange careers – they were mostly young, rather lost, trying to get themselves together. A painter, a craftsman, another who called himself a writer. Here's where wanting to be an artist gets you, a so-called trendy café in the north of Paris, serving cappuccinos and Caesar salads. What didn't change was the way they made up for it, at the end of their shift, with Picon beer and cocaine. Getting high was a constant.

They would talk about football or the hot girl someone was screwing. They put powder up their noses, like on the boulevard Saint-Michel, and everywhere else probably. Humanity's chains made of cheeseburgers and gin and tonics.

They exploit you, they exhaust you with their brunches and birthday dinners, they make you run with pints in your hands and you become an idiot, a total zombie, in a trendy café in northern Paris: since they came here the painter had stopped painting and the writer had stopped writing, and Tobias was growing apart from Victor. On the other hand, there was still alcohol, and there were still drugs.

Youth gets crushed one gratuity at a time; time is always out of joint when you get up at three in the afternoon to resume your life. So why wouldn't they take drugs when life is so dull? It's their choice, but can you blame them for running a mile from neon-lit offices and luncheon vouchers?

The only consolation is, you don't have to set the alarm clock, because at 6 p.m., the shift is back like a crack of the whip, and a day begins that will last until 4 o'clock in the morning. You rush around, you smile, you bring menus and baskets of bread. You work on autopilot, not thinking, and yet you would be almost happy to be there in a so-called hip café in northern Paris – because there are hot girls, because you can listen to deafening music at work, because the customers dress like you. And yet, you're just a little piece of shit doing their bidding. A jug of water, and as fast as you can. There must be masters and slaves. Is there really a dialectic? The slave serves, the master orders, but then what?

Tobias no longer went to meet Victor at his grey office on the avenue du Maine. He was either working or, when he had a day off – or rest day, if you prefer – he was so happy to be able to do nothing come 6 o'clock that he forgot about Victor and his PR career. It's harder to be in love when you're busy. They had to develop new habits as a couple, unlearn the language they'd spoken till then, as though reality, the trivialities of common people, were festering between them and gradually pulling them apart.

While Tobias was at work, Victor waited for him at home alone. He got bored. At first, he was happy just waiting; he'd fall asleep, leaving space for him in the middle of the mattress. Then he got tired of falling asleep like that, pointlessly. So he went back to his habits as a single man – talons out, in search of pleasure, in orgy bars.

He only went to look. Naked, copulating bodies paraded in front of him. Victor masturbated for a while, and then went home, thinking of Tobias. But as the weeks went by, he spent longer in the bars, talking, glass in hand, surrounded by all those taut, muscled bodies.

His desires banished the image of Tobias, as though his eyelids had made him disappear. He touched the men who danced in front of him, he took them with force, as he used to, slipping from one to another – the strange carnal merry-go-round that keeps spinning till you're dizzy, until you feel sick.

He caught the bad flu, among all those bodies he'd had. He sensed it. He knew instantly. He didn't tell anyone, he wanted to omit that from his life.

He didn't think about the harm he could do; he continued living as though he'd really forgotten what he had in his blood.

As Tobias and Victor drifted further apart, the months sped by increasingly quickly.

They had some happy times, of course: a weekend in the country, evenings with friends.

But there was no understanding between Tobias and Victor any more. An argument that was no more serious than all the rest decided their separation.

As a final twist of the knife, Victor told Tobias what he had inside him, what he'd given him; that he'd marked him with a branding iron. He'd done for him.

V

Armand and Emma often took the metro together. In the morning she'd come and collect him from outside his mother's on the way to school. They'd kiss on the flip-up seats, cut off from the daylight, among the other passengers. It was their thing, in the tunnels, in the corridors or carriages, as though they were divorced from the rest of the world, lit by the neon lights of the tunnels.

They drank coffee, too, at Le Rouquet on the boulevard Saint-Germain. They smoked together, they kissed, and felt contempt for other people. They were better than them. They'd found each other; they would never part.

In ten years, if they were no longer together, they would meet, on 6 June at 8.15 in the evening in front of the church on the boulevard Saint-Germain.

She had a white coat. Armand wore ties and ripped jeans. They were falling in love. He was sixteen and she was seventeen.

Armand no longer wanted to be apart from Emma; he left his mother's without saying goodbye to live in the little apartment in La Muette. He had passed the first part of his bac and she'd got the second, the real one, which launches you into adult life.

They stayed in bed, in the little two-room in La Muette, happily fucking and smoking, under the quilt. Sometimes they sat on the tiny zinc balcony.

Armand would go out for a few hours to cadge smokes from strangers, then he'd come back with his pockets stuffed with loose cigarettes. They ate pasta or rice. They didn't need money, since they were in love, in the little two-room apartment in La Muette on the floor above Emma's grandmother.

That summer they went to a luxury hotel in Deauville for five days. Emma's father had received an invitation and gave his daughter four nights in the hotel as a gift. Emma and Armand felt proud arriving at the hotel reception. They laid waste to the minibar and room service.

In the afternoons they went walking on the beach, like the old couples they despised.

Sometimes Armand went down to the hotel bar alone for a gin and tonic while Emma was asleep. He liked the thought of how he looked. When he wasn't with her, he observed himself living, and he liked his image. He was in love, he was handsome, he was young, too young to live the way he was. He cultivated his contradictions, like the ties with ripped jeans. That's also what he loved about Emma, she wasn't predictable. She was one of those people you can't work out immediately. She epitomised in his eyes the out-of-place middle-class girl, the modern version of corrupt aristocracy. He liked not being able to fathom her, with her little-rich-girl habits and semi-bohemian lifestyle. He liked those paradoxes, talking about anarchy in the bar of a luxury hotel in Deauville; the idea that you can feel comfortable with ordinary people because of your ideas and the upper classes because of your manners; a permanent disjunction that means you don't belong anywhere. You are unfathomable, 'never explain, never complain', but have an innate ease. They lived like no one else.

Armand enjoyed seeing this paradox deepen. His school friends couldn't understand how he could live with a girl, adults were baffled too, seeing them living like them. He felt as though he wasn't part of society even as he walked around in it. This feeling made him joyful beyond measure. He was observing his own existence.

When they got back from Deauville, they had to leave the little apartment in La Muette. Armand found an attic in rue du Quatre Septembre. They stayed there two years, joined at the hip, covering the meagre rent thanks to their fathers. Armand bought a scooter, a Honda Scoopy SH50, with red plastic trim. At last he was free; he had a room, a scooter and a girl to love.

At school he seemed to be living in another world. It looked easy, but he was short of money. He gave some private lessons, but that wasn't enough. He had to find a way of getting by so as not to lose face with Emma. He learned to steal, not expensive things, just food and shampoo, beer and Mentos from the local mini-market.

He learned to ask for things too.

Near school there was a café where all the students had lunch. Serge ran the place. He was a good guy. Every day he gave Armand his lunch and pretended to get him to pay without other people noticing.

Emma worked at her preparatory classes for university. Armand rode around on his scooter, stealing books or food, then returned to their attic, happy to find her waiting for him.

Armand passed his bac, as Emma had done a year earlier, and began his first year of prep for university. They worked on their lessons, they slept together. But something was missing, something of the enthusiasm they had had in sharing their normal life.

VI

Franz was eighteen when he arrived in Berlin. He had his bag in his hand, the wedding suit and his diploma from the Hannover Institute. Sir had recommended him to a few businesses in the city – in the west, where the streets are cleaner, the people busy, like in Munich, and the economy thriving. The men walk quickly, holding sandwiches, as though they couldn't possibly waste time on lunch. The women – both young and old – clack their heels energetically. They look proud and powerful. You wonder how they pick up men. Maybe they go for men more powerful than them; or less, and dominate them with a few little slaps.

Franz liked all this activity. Between their offices and the luxury shops, these people were in a hurry, preoccupied, and how happy they must be, since they had no time to idly nurture their little neuroses.

After attending a few interviews wearing his tie, Franz entered this world. He was to be executive assistant at Günther and Co. After all, being an assistant is not so bad if 'executive' is part of your title, he thought. You start as a secretary and you climb the ladder, a lifelong career at Günther and Co.

He started work. It was dull. And his company's offices were gloomy, too. But that's how it goes, you get a boring job at Günther and Co, slog your guts out, then one day you marry a Katherine, with a hollow face and no spark, but soft skin and gleaming hair. You make love and a little Martin comes along. You go on holiday in your car. Before long, Martin will graduate and you can relax.

Meanwhile, Franz lived in a two-room apartment in Nollendorfplatz. He was eighteen. He did the filing. In the evening, he closed the door and read second-hand books.

VII

Tobias didn't know what to do. He schlepped all over, in the metro, squats, parks. He soon left the café where he was working; then it was heroin and that whole life. Not for long, just a month, until fate reached out to him.

He was walking along the rue de Tocqueville, looking at the ground, hoping to spot a coin or a handkerchief, something to catch his attention. But rather than a scratch card or a banana skin, he spotted his sister's shoes. He looked up – yes, it was her, like an apparition, with a little boy by her side.

There were no benches nearby, so they went to a café. His sister was alarmed at how pale Tobias was. But it wasn't the moment to think about that, they were back together again; and at last he was able to meet her son, little Lucas.

Lucas looked impressed as he drank his grenadine.

'Lucas, this is my brother, Tobias, your uncle.'

Tobias was ashamed of the state he was in: pale and dirty. He was sorry he hadn't met his nephew a few months earlier when he was working, when he was in love.

He thought about life's setbacks, but this one had worked in his favour. His sister took him in. He detoxed in the little apartment on the rue Campagne-Première, where he lived with his sister and Lucas. Stéphane had got a promotion to London. He'd gone. They were separated.

Life on rue Campagne-Première was nice. As before, Tobias made the soup, but now he wasn't alone during the day, he looked after Lucas. He took him to the park, bought him waffles.

In the evening, his sister came back from the grind. They put the child to bed and read him a story. Then Tobias and his sister would sit in the lounge. They talked about all the years when they hadn't seen each other, and how they'd changed.

To put some distance between him, the drugs and his memories, his sister decided to find something for Tobias to do, a nice job, away from Paris.

A job as a translator had come up in Berlin. Tobias would have an apartment and a salary. He'd leave the following week.

This prospect frightened him. He didn't know anyone in Berlin; he'd never lived there. He'd have to start from scratch once more, make links, find bars, try above all to feel German again. Even with his sister he spoke French, and now he'd have to rediscover the language of his childhood.

He'd grown fond of Lucas; he'd be leaving him

too as well as all his habits. Tobias was afraid, but he was full of drive. Remaking himself, being reborn, that was what this was about. Trying to stand on his own two feet, as though he had never needed crutches.

The goodbyes were painful. Lucas cried, he tightened up his fists and then let go, as though he knew that with only the strength of a child he couldn't stop Tobias going.

All three of them took the bus to the airport. Tobias was carrying a small bag, all that he had left, a few pullovers and a cap. His mother had bought him the cap in New York when he arrived. It was the only thing he'd never lost. People move on, caps remain.

Yes, caps remain if you ram them on your head firmly enough.

The bus was busy. People sweating as they set off or returned. Tobias felt a stranger among all these holidaymakers, these school holiday adventurers. He wasn't going to take a few Polaroids of a new city, he was changing his life; you don't take photos of your normal life, you don't want to remember the everyday.

At the airport he kissed his sister and little Lucas, who was in floods of tears.

As he went towards the security gate, he thought about his new life. But almost at once a feeling overtook him; he was doomed and he would carry that with him whatever he did.

VIII

Armand liked Emma's intelligence because of the particular feeling it gave him; he couldn't bluff with her, she understood him, she always would. But after a while, he no longer felt flattered by her intelligence. Emma understood him; she understood him too well. She had grasped him as a whole, he was a whole without mystery. She could spot his little lies immediately, his little embroidered lies that reshape stories in the telling, to make them funnier or stranger. What annoyed Armand was not that Emma no longer held any mystery for him, he hadn't noticed that. What annoyed him more, though he couldn't have put it into words, was feeling entirely understood, no longer seeing her eyes shining with admiration when he told her a story. She couldn't be his fan any more since she had understood him. Armand felt hollow, like a man without secrets, an empty man.

He was smoking a cigarette in a bar when he met Louise. It was a huge pleasure to be able to refashion his character. She was beautiful; she had that rare unselfconscious beauty. She looked at him wide-eyed, as though she wanted to touch him. Armand existed again. Louise was a fan of the character he thought he was.

Without saying goodbye, he left Emma; he went with Louise to the Greek islands, where moist bodies take pleasure in intertwining.

He was proud of Louise's beauty, since he possessed it, and the men around her couldn't take their eyes off her.

When they got back to Paris, Louise rode around on the back of his scooter as Emma had done, but he didn't think about her, because he was absorbed by pretty Louise. At least she didn't understand him yet.

Then Louise went back to her country and Armand found a little room on rue Oberkampf. He'd given up his studies to devote himself to painting. He thought that would only last a year.

IX

Franz met Martha. Martha Krüll, a pastor's daughter. She was a year older than him, blonde, and her face possessed the radiance which Katherine's had lost. Grace, that was it, Martha had inner grace. Venus-like, she passed though life as though it were a quest for purity. He was under the arcades of the overhead metro track, when he saw her go by and immediately grasped her appeal. She was on her own, without any obvious destination. Instinctively, he followed her for a while, without considering the consequences. The closer he got to her, the more he felt the grace that emanated from her, as though it had entered his heart.

He approached her awkwardly. Martha could have ignored him or called him a lout, but she looked at Franz and saw in him what she had long been looking for: a good, sincere man, lost perhaps, but life-saving. A decent man standing in front of her under the girders of the overhead metro track.

'I saw you go by and followed you. It's uncivilised, maybe, but I had to. We have something in common. I feel it, I'm sure of it. I'd like to see you again. Will you give me your number?'

'My diary's full of numbers. They're piling up. What are you doing tomorrow?'

'Tomorrow? I don't know. It's Saturday. I don't know.'

'We can meet back here if you like. At three. We can go to a café. I'm Martha. Martha Krüll.'

'Nice to meet you, Martha. See you tomorrow.'

He went off. What an idiot, he thought, I didn't even tell her my name. He turned round to go after her, but she had already gone.

Never mind. He'd make up for it tomorrow. Oh Martha, Martha. He treasured her name as if he were already able to love her.

Martha. Martha Krüll. What an idiot he'd been not to tell her his. Franz. Franz Riepler. Nothing to be ashamed of.

They met again at three the following day. Franz hadn't brought flowers. That wasn't his style. But then it wasn't his style to accost girls in the street. But here he was, ready to love her, and isn't that better than pulling up some plants?

They went to one of those cafés you find everywhere in Germany, well-heated, with armchairs and low tables with ashtrays on them. The kind of place where you linger for several hours. In Berlin there aren't cafés you just drop in to; if you're in a hurry, you drink your coffee from a paper cup as you go.

The conversation took off. There was something obviously right about being there, ensconced in the velvet armchairs, face to face. Franz and Martha understood each other in a way that few people can.

There was a sequence of these café visits, and then came the pleasures of the flesh, with the same sense of rightness, the same simplicity.

Martha slept at Franz's. Gradually she left her things there, then stayed there all the time, to feel closer to him. Franz was still working at Günther and Co. A serious guy, that's what they said about him. But his life began in the evening when he was back with pretty Martha. Martha with her honey-coloured eyes, her pale skin, her radiant face.

Their love became platonic, but still they felt satisfied.

It lasted two years, and then it was as though the system broke down. They disentangled themselves and decided to go their separate ways. Martha went back to her father, Pastor Krüll. Franz went as far away as he could, all the way to Mexico.

X

Schönefeld Airport seemed very strange to Tobias. He understood the words on the signs, but they resonated subconsciously, like a language he had forgotten.

He took the S-Bahn and then the U-Bahn – ah, so that's what they call the metro! *Zazie in the U-Bahn* doesn't have such a ring to it.

He had to report to the office where he was going to work – that was the priority; his sister had given him some money, but it wouldn't last long – once again, he needed to earn his living. What a strange expression that seems when you're sad, when your soul wants to wander and your body is sick.

On the U-Bahn the passengers' faces were different – it was subtle rather than striking, but he felt in the depths of his being that he was no longer at home. It's not just what you see, of course; what you hear doesn't have meaning for you either, so you look and listen like a naturalist. The three notes of the closing train doors sound like a melody. You don't understand that the train is about to depart; it's different from the metro. He checks the stations as he goes. Ah, they've put maps on the ceiling, there's an idea, very practical. Plätenwald, Treptower Park, Ostkreuz. Yes, change at Ostkreuz and then take the U6 line to Alexanderplatz. Alexanderplatz, that was what the boss said in his letter. The translation bureau is impossible to miss; it's at the bottom of the TV tower opposite McDonald's. What does this TV tower look like? It seems it's completely straight, like a cock that's been stuck on the city. Ah, we're coming out of the tunnels. The sky's so grey here. No sun or clouds. And buildings, so shiny and low! It's a far cry from Baron Haussmann's embellishments. Everything looks like it has a use. It's sad all the same, a city where everything is useful. What about poetry, where do they put that? Maybe they've made little parking lots for sonnets and hangars and factories for ballads.

The S-Bahn train follows its route, a succession of waste ground, industrial units and a scattering of apartment blocks. At least they don't seem short of space. There's something galactic in the air. It's not a city to stroll around. But what is he going to do, since the only thing he likes is walking? Maybe it's not all like this; after all, this is the route from the airport – he's still a long way from the city centre. No, hold on, here's Ostkreuz on the map. So this is it, he *is* in the heart of Berlin! So where are the shops and the workers, the scooters and the bakeries? People here look like they do as they're told. Sometimes they go for a walk in a car park full of poetry.

Charm is what Tobias is after. Soon he'll discover that here beauty is to be found among people and the way they live, and not as in Paris on facades and on the pavements.

'Hello, I'm Tobias Kent. I've got an appointment with Mr Peter.'

'Wait here, I'll let him know.'

Tobias waited in a little dark room, like a dentist's waiting room with four regularly spaced chairs – no danger of your arm brushing against your neighbour's – a glass-topped coffee table and of course piles of magazines – news, sport, women's fashion – humanity divided into three categories. Like in Paris, you are either a woman, a sportsman or a man of the world. So what should Tobias read?

'Mr Kent? Christian Peter will see you now.'

Tobias got up, thinking about his new life.

He had to translate instruction manuals into English, German and French. It wasn't too badly paid – from Monday to Friday, eight till five with a lunch break.

A life of spewing out copy; this was new to Tobias. But it would enable him to live

– apparently that comes at a price. This would be his, from Monday to Friday, eight till five, with a lunch break.

Tobias would have a small wooden desk with a shiny top. Mr Peter was insignificant, and nothing need be said of the secretary.

Christian Peter could put a studio flat 'at Tobias's disposal', as he put it. The rent would be deducted from his salary.

Tobias took the flat. It wasn't too far from the office; U2 from Alexanderplatz to Schönhauser Allee. There was also a tram, as Tobias would discover later. The underground is reassuring when you don't know a city – all undergrounds are alike, there's no scenery.

At the exit from the U-Bahn, there was a big shopping centre unlike anything in Paris. The people seemed to be strolling around or drinking coffee from cardboard cups. A bit of bustle outside the shopping centre, someone selling Wurst, workers waiting for the tram, and then on the left, 72d, the building where he was going to live. It looked more like the kind of suburban block that has a fancy name; at number 72 there were four blocks which shared a courtyard full of bikes, 72a, 72b, 72c, 72d.

Tobias took his little bag up to the first floor. One of those typical Berlin staircases with a big wooden handrail and lino-covered floor – a plasticky smell and the warmth of the building. You sense the winters here are hard, people are used to protecting themselves.

The apartment was comfortable. Tobias would sort it out, construct what he liked to think of as a little nest, a shelter from other people, from their smell and their failures. Here Tobias would cook and read – he would live alone, and have nothing to do with sex bars and drugs. He was sick of them. It would be good to be a new man, a man with an ordinary face. He wanted to open up a little path for himself, only for himself, without detours and misunderstandings. He was hoping for a nice middle-class life. He didn't want to feel ashamed any more when he took the underground in the morning; he would go to work, no thoughts in his head. He wanted to melt into the little world around him. Peace. He wanted to live like other people.

XI

Armand enjoyed striking an attitude: alone, melancholy and devoted to his painting. He smoked roll-ups and cherished his feeling of restlessness as the only thing that couldn't be taken away from him. He crumbled cheap resin in the palm of his hand and thought about his woes as he listened to singers with gravelly voices. He hung around in cafés, scribbling a few sketches in a moleskin notebook. He tried to catch girls' eyes and look proud of his solitude. There were always men around but he didn't talk to them, so he felt this artificial solitude permanently assailing him from outside. He thought about it and displayed it like a conquest. He portrayed himself as withdrawn from the world, a lonely, hungry painter.

Autumn arrived and soon it was November, the most beautiful month for melancholia. As a result of displaying his sadness, Armand came to believe in it. He lost his sense of humour.

During the day he worked as a supervisor in a high school, and in the evenings, since he was no longer painting, he drank beer and smoked weed.

He watched himself walk, so he thought, *the solitary path of his destiny.*

But he wasn't really so isolated; he'd go walking

with his old friends, the fraternity he'd chosen, and they'd all smoke cheap resin and talk about their melancholia and the imaginary woman they'd like to fall in love with.

The little band of lost boys met at Armand's place or in a bar, to smoke or drink, to do something, to talk, have a laugh.

At first, Armand enjoyed these affectations of despairing youth, but he quickly came to believe them to such an extent that they became banal. He wanted to escape them but couldn't, the habit had got under his skin.

He read all day at his job at the school. Mid-century authors who, like him, had just one obsession: finding a place in the world, a role to play in life. He discovered Bove, Calet, Dabit and Hyvernaud, Guérin and Calaferte. But he loved Charles-Louis Philippe more than them all. Then, he imagined himself contracting syphilis at the start of last century – it was certainly classier than AIDS – falling for a tart from the boulevard Sébastopol, living a bohemian life in a brothel, as a small-time dealer in vague artistic desires. He felt nostalgic for an era he'd never known; he envied that type of poverty for being much more romantic than his little part-time job in a Catholic high school.

Yes, he worked in a Catholic high school; the ultimate anarcho-betrayal, a religious institution of the state that was authoritarian and repressive. But it earned him some money and all he did was read and smoke.

Sometimes he painted. Then he felt the return of the strength he'd been lacking. It would make him forget, stop him watching himself living. His thoughts exploded. Hunched over his canvases, he used his brush as though he were jabbing a wall – he was living for himself at last. He forgot his pose and found his inner self, so close to his gut that he could smell his own shit. He spewed forth his judgement.

From time to time, he screwed a pick-up from the bar. And then he felt calmer for a few days.

It was in mid-winter that Emma's shadow came to haunt his vision. She cast a veil over his eyes, the pretty Dunhill blonde. Since he was tired of envying periods of history he had never known, he returned to his own past.

He'd been so happy when he was in love with her! He understood now that he wasn't made to be alone. He needed to be entwined with a woman, specifically Emma.

He thought about seeing her again, but didn't

call. Perhaps he was ashamed of his cowardice, of how he'd left her. When things went on too long, he couldn't stop himself running away. He could have thought 'fuck it', but the memories of the mean things he'd done hit him like a big block of guilt.

He was ashamed, his body felt sick. To get rid of it, he ran away again.

XII

Franz drank a lot in Mexico. And there were joints, crappy dancing, nights when you tried to forget yourself. There were conquests in bars, and then it was time to go home; the date printed on the plane ticket had come round already.

When he got back, he had an irresistible urge to see Martha. You don't forget a woman you have loved after just a few glasses of warm beer.

The pastor was away, so Franz was able to visit Martha at home. He was touched by the sight of her childhood room, her serious soft toys, the little bed where she'd had her nightmares. They made love, hurriedly, as a sort of way of saying goodbye. Then Franz went back to his apartment, his life as a single man, the Günther and Co. files, the second-hand books, the whole thing.

Mexico had left a taste for adventure at the back of his throat. He wanted to resume his studies, fashion design, a school in Paris. His application was accepted; in two months he'd be off.

The plan was perfect. Escape. Except Franz had forgotten destiny, the old enemy who grabs you by the shoulder. Martha was pregnant. She wanted to keep this child, Franz's child. Martha, Martha Krüll, the pastor's daughter, would not have an abortion; that was out of the question.

XIII

For the first time, Tobias had arrived in a new city alone. He knew no one; he couldn't use his mother's or sister's apartment as an anchor. There was only 72d on Schönhauser Allee, a little impersonal one-bedroom place, a testament to his solitude. But because he was truly alone, because the faces around him did not look at him, he didn't experience it like that.

The simplest things had a particular appeal because he was doing them for the first time. His disorientation kept him busy. He didn't know what to buy in the supermarket; he didn't know what to do with underground tickets. It was as though he were a stranger to the pact with the city; he had to discover its customs. So he walked around, eyes wide open, trying to understand, to blend into indifference. He developed a little repertoire of the ways things were done; people here didn't cross when the red man was on or walk on cycle paths.

He rediscovered the language of his childhood more easily than he expected.

When he wasn't working, he walked the streets and travelled the tunnels of the U-Bahn. He visited museums and monuments. Occasionally he went to the cinema.

He loved being in this state of discovery. He walked instinctively since he needed to understand, and above all create new habits. Maybe that's why he started smoking again, so that he could go to the same kiosk every day, and the old Turkish man who ran it would reach for the packet of Blue Nile from behind him without Tobias even asking.

He didn't worry about running into friends or lovers; he wanted to make a life for himself as a solitary man with his work, his cigarettes, his supermarket.

The work was unappealing; Tobias couldn't have asked for better. He translated instruction manuals for machines he'd never use. It was a world he didn't need to think about, he just made his little contribution.

His apartment was coming together. He cut photos out of newspapers and stuck them on the walls; headlines, too, when he liked them. Titles in block capitals and funny little items of news: '72-year-old eaten by her cats'; 'he smothered his grandmother because she confiscated his PlayStation'.

Sometimes he received a letter from his sister. Little Lucas signed at the bottom right in his shaky handwriting. The weeks went by uneventfully, between the instruction manuals and 72d, between his discoveries and the habits he was forming.

But there came a point when Tobias was no longer making discoveries; he had a season ticket for the underground, the old Turkish man instinctively handed him his packet of Blue Nile every morning, he knew the supermarket shelves.

The day he realised this, Tobias was struck by a great sense of sadness. He felt stunned. What was he to do now that he had his habits nicely arranged around him? Should he content himself with observing them, all these little independent actions, so independent that they functioned by themselves, like motorised creatures that didn't need anyone guiding them? He had polished them so well, held them so tight between his palms, that it was as though all these little everyday habits existed outside him. Enthusiasm for the ritual one has created can be destroyed by the sadness of the habit. And amid all these stale attractions, Tobias was getting bored.

He remembered a tract from the Lettrist movement which Jérôme had read to him one evening: *The adventurer is someone who makes adventures happen, rather than someone to whom adventures happen.*

XIV

Perhaps Armand wanted to get away so that he could stop thinking about Emma and create a new personality for himself, far from his past.

He could choose a new character, escape the role he'd played with his friends. He would only be able to forget that role if he left them and went off to something entirely new.

Perhaps he'd go to Rome or Berlin; for now, he made do with talking about it. Departures had style; he would be accountable to no one, he could live out his idiosyncrasies as he saw fit. He'd be free, he wouldn't have the incessant gaze of those around him weighing him down. Since he could not free himself from them while they were around, he would escape.

How would he live? He didn't have the slightest idea. Never mind, he'd always managed somehow. That sort of detail wasn't worth getting hung up on. He'd put a bit of money aside; he'd be frugal for a few months. Then what? Then, time would tell.

He got a job in the bar downstairs from his flat. He worked there in the evenings; during the day he was a school supervisor. Now, when Armand thinks back on that time, he remembers the lack of sleep and the smell of the metro. He got exhausted going from one job to another, and meanwhile he was thinking about his departure.

Before he left, he wanted to see Emma again. They spent the night in his little bare room, as he had already packed away all his things in a friend's cellar. They did some coke, and slept on the little mattress he used as a bed. He smelled her skin on the thin mattress and he swore he would leave and never come back.

It was summer. Armand chose Berlin. He bought a budget ticket. It was so strange buying it just one-way!

A few days later, he set off to live his new life. He was twenty.

He was so preoccupied by tiny details of style that he forgot to feel afraid. He didn't know where he was going to sleep; he had a bit of money in his pocket and a bag with a few things.

XV

Franz abandoned his thoughts of adventure. He took a job in a bar in the evenings in addition to his hack work in the office. He needed space, and money for little Juli, who was on the way.

Franz could no longer read his books with the yellowing pages. Fate had caught up with him and he had to march to its tune.

Juli was born. Juli Riepler. It was a joyful moment for them all, for Martha, for Pastor Krüll, and Franz too.

Life was organised with confidence. They created a warm, pink room for Juli at the pastor's house. Martha took care of it, along with the nappies and the feeds. Franz worked, he paid his share, and as soon as he was free, he picked Juli up in his arms, thanking that friend, Fate, whom he had hated a few months earlier, when he had grabbed him by the shoulder.

In the bar where he worked, Franz was often asked if he knew someone to buy from. He didn't understand at first. Buy what from? Drugs, of course.

Months went by; sometimes he took them. Then, he made some good contacts. Juli was getting bigger; he needed more money. Franz became a dealer on the side to earn a bit more. Ecstasy and amphetamines made a good profit. It was a far cry from the nine-to-five.

Business flourished; Franz got bigger. People liked him because he didn't cut the product too much.

Those were the salad days, of plenty of money and freedom. He had come a long way from Günther and Co. and the cocktail bar. He was his own boss; he sold to nightclub dealers who came to his apartment every week to stock up. Little Juli, raised on drug money. Every line done in a nightclub toilet, every pill swallowed meant a bit of comfort for Juli, money for her education, a new teddy.

Then, as always in these stories, Franz got caught. Police. House search. Clink.

XVI

Tobias tried to see things outside so-called normal life. He went to sex bars and *druffi* nightclubs. He went back to the life he managed best wherever he was, the drug addict. He became friends with his neighbour on the second floor who offered him his couch. He gave up the instruction manuals and the apartment that went with them.

The eternal return. His life resumed its original cycle. For him, this was normal life.

XVII

Two years in prison leaves its traces on a man's face: marks of submission, fear and humiliation. Franz did two years, since he was unable to hold out and grassed up his suppliers, some Poles, who were much bigger fish than him.

When he got out, he wanted to work. No one would take him on; his face was puffy with the marks of jail. Juli no longer recognised him; he couldn't buy her a new teddy any more. He was done.

He did a few jobs on a rehabilitation programme, scraping posters off walls, checking tickets on the U-Bahn. He gambled the money he made in slot machines. Most of the time he won. He doubled his stakes, tiny amounts.

He was able to see Juli, Martha and Pastor Krüll again. He tried putting make-up on the lines on his face. What would Katherine, Sir and Madam have thought if they'd seen him in this state? The Institute's uniform was falling to pieces, it no longer covered his body.

Franz partied on. At least in that world no one asked him questions about the lines on his face. At parties that went on for days, that existed outside time, his past didn't matter.

The *druffis* welcomed him. They gave him tobacco and put him up. They were his family now.

PART TWO

'Door Closes Automatically'

Berlin

There is something so new about Berlin it's frightening. The walls of the apartment blocks are not burdened with stones, but poured from concrete, smooth or rough-cast, like the slabs between the windows of apartments. Here, apartment blocks are not like women lying down or standing up, but seated, neither tall nor short; they don't offer you their thighs, but simply remain there, at rest. It would be hard to know what to say to these women without realising they are the product of a terrible history, that they have been seated there, on these broad armchairs, so that they can once again welcome men freed from their demons. Since they provide warmth cheaply, little groups of artists take refuge in them. They don't create anything, but it doesn't matter; they live, going from one space to another, picking up furniture that they find on the pavement. They go cycling, their children following on their little bicycles without pedals, alternately balancing their little legs against the ground. In winter, when the pavements are snow-covered, the children are pulled along in sledges with a piece of string, like Inuits.

These children look happy since people have time to take care of them, and their parents' faces suggest they are carefree too.

The streets are wide and people walk around, as though nothing could happen to them, as if here more than elsewhere people take time to live. People are a bit skint but they get by. The soups are good. People smoke in the cafés since it would be crazy not to. They work away on a laptop at some obsession. You sense Europe is around you, all its languages mixing and answering each other.

Idleness is king. Sometimes, it ruins men; excess hollows the cheeks of those who don't have to get up in the morning, the dark circles round their eyes look carved in. Some party until they can take no more – there is always somewhere open here to welcome them. It liberates some and crushes others. Freedom demands strength; some are weak and quickly lose their way. But around them, others continue with their bike rides, their tram journeys and their nice lives. It's simple enough; these are men whom Work has not crushed. This is a situationist city.

I

Since he was going to experience new things, Armand felt that he should write about them. He took a small black notebook and slipped it into his pocket along with a pen. When he was alone, he would make a sort of record of his existence.

A notebook for Berlin. Write down a thought, a story, a joke every day (one page, as a discipline). I'm leaving tomorrow. There are some things I shall miss; but my excitement has the upper hand. Today, writing emails and carting things around, a scooter too. Leave the fewest traces possible, not contacting E or L. Leave alone, without ties, because that is ultimately what I wanted. A little adventure with all my twenty years of wisdom.

Don't make a song and dance of it, though. I'm going to live somewhere else, but like here; there's nothing very disorientating about it. The language maybe, the signs, the street names and surnames, which I'll have to decipher letter by letter like in primary school. Some customs will be different but maybe no more than in another district in Paris.

I'll no longer be at home and I can hardly wait. The streets will have no associations; I shall have to construct new memories.

I'm sitting outside a café opposite V's place, V

who offered me his couch; the horrible rue de Babylone where I've had so many different experiences. Over there, all that will end. I understand why people talk about a fresh start.

All the threads I have woven will disappear, that's a therapeutic virtue.

Where will I be this time tomorrow? In a street with an unpronounceable name, in a café again. That would be good.

Where will I sleep tomorrow? No idea. In a bed probably. Places change; the same things happen. That's no surprise really. It's reassuring. But also troubling. So that's life. That is how all future days will go. Cafés and a mattress at the end, alone or with a girl. Every night I'll sleep on a bed or a sofa, on the ground, in the dirt. There is no surprise, no surprise parcel to open.

Yes there is: death. Talk about a surprise!

It's the first day of the autumn term. I'm leaving. People in the street are rushing about, thinking about the new (academic/office) year. Their arms are full of new things and their heads are buzzing. A new timetable, a squared A4 notebook. Same old shit.

They look happy to be resuming the course of their lives. I'm leaving, and you won't be seeing me again.

I only despise them insofar as I'm like them.

They come from Bon Marché, carrying big orange handbags and wearing really expensive perfume. Rive gauche. That isn't mine. No, it's not my element. I may like it nonetheless, the women are prettier there.

Does Berlin have a Left Bank?

So many lives I will not touch, that I'll never understand. We want to write about men.

As if it were a matter of experiencing something, we leave, tail first.

When Armand arrived in Berlin, it was raining. The grey dome over the city was spitting out its regularly spaced phlegm. It was almost possible to believe that you could avoid the raindrops by darting between them. The sky is mocking you, that's an omen. Armand's sky was rainy but intangible, the sort of rain that doesn't soak your head. But at some point a fat drop forms and hits the tip of your cigarette with its full weight. Sometimes, with a bit of luck, you just end up smoking something slightly damp, but other times, fate strikes so hard and so accurately that the cigarette has had it. You take a drag, and all you get is a sappy taste through the filter. You light up another and life goes on. Nothing has changed; but it's there, the little taste of artificial sap tickling your throat. At least there is that nice sound, the *psst* of water on the tip, like when you toss a butt in a plastic cup at a student party. It's one blini among many, a toast to be savoured.

Armand was walking through the raindrops, a new cigarette between his lips. He'd got off the plane and collected his bag. That weighed him down a bit but not too much; it was very flimsy material from which to construct a new life: some books, a computer, trousers and a pair of shoes.

He thought about taking a taxi. But what address would he have given? He'd take the underground. At least you could trust it; there were maps, a vague idea of the city – the names of stations. Some inspire trust and others don't. Armand's drift through Berlin would be psychogeographical. He wanted to lug his bag where his spirit led him, follow streets that would inspire him, avoid others, no regrets, and never go back.

He took the S-Bahn, watched the passengers, counted stations. He'd get off at Mehringdamm; he'd been told that Kreuzberg was a nice area.

When he came out of the U-Bahn, it was still raining, still morning. Armand was hungry. He took shelter under the frontage of a fast food joint. Enthusiastically, he ate a hamburger alone, right up at the restaurant window, watching the rain. The scene should have been desperately sad, but Armand liked it; he was free, no one watching him, in a new city.

The rain was easing off nicely. Armand put down his tray on one of the trolleys that a cleaner would have to move later. He left the burger joint.

He walked for a bit. Then, as it was still raining, he found a café. He ordered an espresso and a croissant. The barman realised he was French.

Armand went to the room upstairs, where you could smoke.

Arrived in Berlin today. It's raining. Finally found a café where you can smoke. It's not unpleasant. Four blondes bedside me. I should describe it better, but what's the point since this notebook is only for me?

Just because, for form's sake; a purely personal aesthetic; a way of imagining one's existence; nothing more. Yes, it may be as simple as that, imagining the aesthetic direction of my own life.

This place is quite nice (the upstairs room, I mean). Smoking, drinking coffee among German girls.

Sense that all my habits (rituals would be more flattering) will be reproduced but without giving me the same feeling. It's different because the places themselves are different.

A nice city where the girls are pretty. Yes, I'm staying, that's for sure. How long I don't know. But I'm definitely staying.

To be able to watch girls smoking in cafés at last!

All afternoon he walked around, forgetting the weight of his existence. When it got dark, he looked for a youth hostel. He had written down some addresses on a piece of paper. He did the rounds. They were all full. Where would he sleep? In the underground?

A friend in Paris had told him about the Berghain, a club that stayed open from Friday till Sunday night. He went there because he didn't know what else to do, because he wasn't tired.

The bouncer didn't look surprised when he turned up with his luggage. Armand went in. Two men searched his bag and his pockets.

He paid his admission, and the Berghain opened before him.

Berghain-Panoramabar

When you come out of the underground, it feels like you're in an industrial district. There's open space, some huts made of sheet metal, ugly apartment blocks fitted with big pink pipes that run along the outside. You still have a few minutes' walk. It's exciting and disagreeable. You prepare yourself for not coming out the same day – you'll dance until you drop. The party will kick off soon. But first, you have to brave the passers-by. They look at you. They know where you're going. They must be able to tell from your face that you haven't slept in twenty-four hours. They're off to do things you never would, off in search of a nice, ordinary Sunday.

In the distance, you can hear the jerky rhythm of robotic music.

The club stands out like a cube of concrete, so grey it's almost beige. The building is colossal; it used to be a factory. At the entrance, people are filtered, then searched. A sign in five different languages says that cameras are forbidden. It's like a military sign.

A huge hall serves as a cloakroom. People rest here too, sitting on sofas. The music is quieter here, you can still talk. Next you have to climb metal staircases.

Then, after the back rooms, the main hall opens before you. On the left are the toilets and on the right a deserted bar. An immense dance floor, with the DJ at the back, *druffis* moving around.

Stroboscopes and green neon lights. The music is brutal. It's mainly gay. Leather and moustaches. Welcome to Berghain.

Higher still, up some more metal staircases, is the Panorama Bar. This space is less impressive. The light is nice, the music more dancy. On the left under the mezzanine are the toilets. Unisex, no mirrors. You wait your turn for a cubicle. Alone, or with a girl, a boy, as many as eight people sometimes. You get high together, in these little metal cubicles, without any greater need to hide than that. Security don't care if several people go in as long as the door is closed.

The taps on the basins are all in a row. You splash water on your face, fill an old beer or Club Mate bottle with water.

In the toilets the music is less loud. Languages mingle. It's a big crowd that knows each other, the same people every Sunday. For nothing in the world would Tobias miss coming here on a Sunday afternoon and getting high.

The room is orientated towards the DJ's cabin. There are big reproductions on the walls. Coloured cubes decorate the ceiling. It's captivating; festive and melancholy. The crowd moves in rhythm, but you can escape it, there's space at the sides.

Big windows behind closed blinds make

up one whole wall of the room. No light from outside filters through. But sometimes at the right moment, as a surprise effect, the shutters open for a few seconds. It causes an enormous burst of pleasure as light surges in for a moment, like a special effect, when the music kicks in and time no longer exists.

II

Armand is dancing; he wouldn't know what else to do. Who could he talk to? He looks around to see what other people are doing. He notes certain movements, adapts them to his style, the style he's trying to give his own body. An arm movement, forward then back, quite simply, like in a race. He's making his way through time like you clock up kilometres in an endurance test. The ecstasy tablets he bought surreptitiously help him keep going, of course, but sometimes he feels time itself sticking to his skin. Hours go by. It's already Sunday morning. The time when people get up and think about eating. Go out and buy croissants for the girl they love.

Armand is all alone. But so is everyone around him. And through their strength as a crowd, they lift the weight of loneliness from him. He's alone, so he dances. The lights are coloured: sparkling reds, blues and yellows. It's an adventure park for the senses. Armand looks at the lights as he dances, with his head up and a smile on his face. The girls are beautiful. He'd like to touch them but his hands are clammy.

When he's tired of dancing, he has a cigarette on one of the couches. Then, keen to fake a sense of composure, he pretends to write a message on his phone. To show all of them, all those eyes without faces, that he is not so lonely since he has someone to text.

He dances some more. God, that red is beautiful; the lights shine. The people around him smile at him. Like all of them, he's happy to be here. It's noon.

A few tracks later, Armand takes an empty bottle he found at his feet and fills it up with water. At the sinks in the toilets, a boy speaks to him in German. Armand doesn't understand, and asks him to say it again in English. The boy is Tobias so he repeats it in French. Armand looks tired, he offers him some speed.

Armand doesn't know it yet, but this is normal here, shared drugs and pleasures, without a second thought. You look tired. I've got some speed; here, take some with me. *Drogensolidarität*.

They lock themselves in a cubicle.

'Are you gay?'

'No.'

'I am, but don't worry, you're not my type. You're new, aren't you? I've not seen you before. It's a small world, you know, us *druffis*.'

'What?'

'*Druffis*. It's a term of endearment for druggies. Party animals, freaks, that lot.'

'Yes, I got here this morning... well, yesterday now.'

'Here, take this and let's dance. I can introduce you to the blonde you've had your eye on. That's Sigrid. She's great. She was the one who asked me to come and speak to you. OK, have you had enough? Come on then, let's dance.'

The two of them make a strange pair in front of the DJ's cabin.

Armand offers half his last ecstasy tab to Tobias.

'Where did you buy it? The E isn't good just now. I'll teach you. Call me Tata, OK? Tata Sarfatti.'

Armand swallows the whole tablet. They both laugh.

'OK, Tata.'

They dance for a few more hours, lose sight of each other, meet up again. Armand kisses Sigrid. They drift apart and get separated. It's hot, the lights seem sweaty, almost fluorescent. The jolting music guides the wayward souls of the Panorama Bar, it's their only mistress, it dictates their movements, a jerky dance, a bodily convulsion. It's an infinite pleasure, synthetic perhaps, but so real that you don't care what caused it. There's nothing as heady as the ecstasy of crowds, crowds of lonely individuals, the *druffis* that Tobias talked about. The girls are easy-going and beautiful; sometimes they'll smile at you and give you a kiss. The bass pounds like your heart, you feel you're living more intensely, with other people. Everyone enjoys it without shame or worry, naked with your pleasure. That pleasure is expressed through raised arms, mouths that sometimes call out. The ketamine heads experience it in slow motion, like in an aquarium; for others, on amphetamines, it's speeded up. It doesn't matter; it's all about your pleasure. No one here begrudges you it.

Armand and Tobias meet again in front of the basins in the toilets. They talk. There's a room for rent in the flat Tobias shares, his WG as they call it here. When they leave here they can take a look. If he likes it, Armand could stay there.

'Have you had any alcohol?'

'Yeah, a few beers,' Armand says.

'No juice for you, then. Next time, I'll give you some. You'll see, it's twenty times better than your shit in capsules.'

Armand's pleasure is wearing off; he's cold, his whole body is shaking. He feels as though he is filled with a thick, scummy wave of exhaustion; the drugs are gradually leaving his system. Abandoned by the pleasure molecules, he looks for Tobias, so they can go and see the room, see it and go to sleep there, burrow under the quilt, sleep, naked, in a soft bed.

He has to find Tobias. What's the time? Eight p.m. already! Time beats down like a big rod.

He has to find Tobias. The Berghain has closed, only the Panorama is still open. That makes the search easier.

He must find Tobias. In the toilets, the freaks are blundering into each other. There's a girl with tattoos who would be pretty if she weren't snapping her jaw at the air. A guy is hitting his head against the wall. Weird convulsions. He is small, bald and blue. He keeps bashing the wall with his head. Beside him is a strange smiling creature, half-boy, half-girl, shaved head, orange eyebrows, mouth crudely extended with lipstick.

He must find Tobias. Ah, there he is! He's tired too. Time to go.

III

The apartment is on Schönhauser Allee in Prenzlauerberg. It's quite a schlep from the Berghain, from the Ostbahnhof. They go on foot nonetheless. For Armand, it's autumn in a new city. He has a sensation of space. Yes, it's that: space and ease. He's following a guy he doesn't know to an apartment to check it out. He's carrying his bag. He's walking towards a new life; he has a heady feeling of disorientation; the wind that's blowing is mild.

Tobias talks incessantly. He hops around. That's how he is when he's on drugs, he has a sense that he's living for what he is. Armand listens. It's reassuring to know he speaks French. Otherwise he might not have gone with him; it's an anchor point.

Tobias is a lot shorter than Armand. It's a bit like he's trotting behind him, and yet he is leading the way. He's talking about a friend who died a few days ago. Drugs, of course. What else would it be in Tobias's circle? Being an addict is a full-time job.

Armand still finds it romantic, how some people make their self-destruction a point of honour, applying themselves to their own decline. He doesn't yet know if drugs will lead to his own disappearance or to living life more fully, but it's a life he wants to taste, life as a shadow.

For now, the streets are broad, the road signs strange and notices impossible to figure out. German words have a particular appeal when you don't understand them, something industrial about the way they are written; the sequences of consonants clustered together; a black language, as though still written in Gothic script. It's a cold kind of sweetness, which envelops you and hits you. Yes, Armand wants to experience this life, these unfamiliar sensations.

The apartment is huge; they all are round here, it's a constant, like the stairways with lino on the floor. The windows go down to the ground. The previous tenant left a week ago, an American who'd stayed six months. His room's available; the other two are Otto's and Claudia's. Tobias has been sleeping on the sofa. It's a stop-gap; he's been here three weeks. Claudia has gone away for a fortnight to see her family in Spain.

A few years back, Otto lived in the apartment with his wife. She left him. Since then, he's rented out rooms to foreigners who are passing through. He's a tall fair-haired guy who comes from the north of Germany. He's a student of history and biology, though he's thirty-five.

He's making dinner. He didn't know if Tobias would be back, but he made extra, just in case. Tobias introduces Armand as a good friend.

Otto invites Armand to stay to dinner. If he likes, he can also stay the night; he looks tired. Tomorrow they can talk about renting the room.

Dinner is fun. They speak English. Armand enjoys the realisation that he's not the same person as when he speaks French. He doesn't have the same character; he doesn't make the same jokes. It's nice to be able to change your identity temporarily.

Armand takes a shower, then falls asleep between clean sheets.

IV

The next morning, as always, there are pancakes and café au lait. The Germans know how to live at home. Maybe because of the harshness of the winters. They have lots of accessories: to froth milk, to keep tea hot, to be comfortable at home without having to go out to the café.

The breakfast is nice. They smoke roll-ups, eat bacon. Tobias and Armand tell Otto about their evening. The three of them are like a family, sitting at the bar in the kitchen.

Otto feels it too. He likes Armand, this young Frenchman who has come here to paint, and why else? Hard to say. Perhaps it's his restlessness that has brought him to this unknown city. He reckons they'll be able to get along, that Armand, because of his youth and his character, will be an ally in the order of his existence. With friends, like in love, you can tell the ones who are going to be on your side.

If Armand likes the room, it's his. The rent is modest; it includes electricity and internet.

Agreed! Armand will live here, put the few possessions he's brought with him in the empty room – it's more reassuring to know they're there than in the Berghain cloakrooms.

They celebrate with another round of pancakes.

According to Tobias, Otto is cool. He gets high too. He was married to a really beautiful girl, an American; but she left because the two of them had got stuck in a rut. Since then, Otto has surrounded himself only with people who are passing through. He chooses foreign flatmates; he's putting Tobias up for a few weeks.

He's a generous guy. Tobias, for example, knew from the time he had problems that he could count on Otto to lend him his sofa and feed him. Yes, he's a truly special guy, Tobias says. I'm pleased the three of us are going to live together; it'll be a good laugh.

V

A white room: tiled walls, tiled floor. A guy in a white coat comes in. Franz is sitting in a hospital chair with armrests.

'O-positive. That's good. Maybe more for us than for you. You're fit, which is good. Just relax. We'll take ten tubes. And afterwards, you can have a sandwich. It takes it out of you, you know…'

'Yes, I know,' Franz replies.

Franz knows the drill. Every month he comes

here to sell his blood. He knows they'll put a tourniquet on high above his elbow and it'll be too tight, that the needle will slide into his vein easily and that the tubes will fill up, one by one, until there are none left.

Then he'll roll down his sleeve, someone will bring him a sandwich, attentively, as though he were ill. The guy on reception will give him a twenty-euro note in a brown envelope and off he'll go with the money in his pocket.

Yes, he knows the drill.

VI

It's dark in the living room. Armand's smoking in an armchair. He sniffs the edge of a yellowed book. These are the only movements permitted by his state of mildly depressive contemplation. He looks as though he's resting after what he's been through, now that he's alone at last. But his features betray a little hint of eagerness, like the adventurer's satisfaction in his new environment. He hasn't yet found the treasure, but he senses it's there, within reach, since he has travelled the whole path. He's a young man at rest.

At the same moment, in an over-the-top rococo basement, Tobias is going from one man to another. He takes and is taken.

Then, for a moment's peace, he locks himself in the toilets. He takes out his syringe and little glass bottle. The liquid rises in the plastic tube. 0.9, 1, 1.1, 1.2, right up to 1.6. A mouthful of Coke, then the contents of the syringe, then another mouthful. He sits on the toilet, his head in his hands. The music filters through, muffled by the toilet doors. He starts to cry. He waits for it to well up within him. He takes out a packet of cigarettes and looks at it for a moment. He breathes deeply, as though he had decided not to look more closely. He puts the bottle and the syringe back in a glasses case, then into his pocket, under his cigarette packet. Tears roll down his face. He strikes his head against the wall, three, four, five times; a little GHB convulsion. He is standing oddly, as though his disorientated body is unsure how to hold him up. His movements are jerky, the instinctive reflexes of muscles in motion. He opens the toilet door. He's going back in. To take and be taken.

In the living room, Armand has fallen asleep by his yellow book. Tobias comes in, looking distracted.

He collapses on the sofa, then falls asleep, fully dressed, as though he's wrecked.

A few moments later, Otto comes out of his room; he sees his two transitory friends and covers them with a thick blanket.

VII

There are lights everywhere, words flashing, numbers jumping out at you with the promise of a new life.

It's one of those little casinos you get in Germany. A far cry from the Côte d'Azur; here there are lots of slot machines and the guy on the door doesn't look at you. You play by pushing big buttons, like in English pubs or on ferries.

A few guys dotted around the place are putting coins in the slots, pressing the illuminated buttons and staring at the screens on their bulky terminals.

Franz is here to gamble the money he got for his blood, his last resources. He's already bought a packet of tobacco so he has sixteen euros left. It's too little to hope for a big win – enough, on the other hand, to increase: for the sixteen to become fifty, the fifty, one hundred and twenty.

He picks his machine. The choice is never straightforward, maybe this one will give you a win, or maybe it'll send you back on to the street, unable even to buy an underground ticket.

Franz has gone with his initial hunch since the time a few months ago when he felt himself drawn, almost as soon as he entered the room, by the machine that went on to spit out the jackpot. Since then he's vowed he'll always trust his instinct.

He sits down. The coins go into the slot as quickly as he earned them, as quickly as his blood filled the tubes. One by one, the tokens disappear, and are lost in the machine. Ten euros gone already. A huge amount when this is all the money you have in the world.

The coins go in. Where do they disappear to? Maybe he should change machine. No, stick with this one. Yes, but what if he loses it all? No, stick with this one. His first instinct.

Two more euros and he's broke. Two euros! It's come to this, wishing he had just one more coin, regretting buying a bit of tobacco.

He's playing more slowly now. There's no rush to gamble your last coins. What will he do if he loses? Go home, to the empty apartment that he's been lent. There's nothing left to eat in the cupboards. His dole is due in a week. What will he do till then? At least he has some tobacco. He'll go and borrow from a friend. He'll make it through the week, but if only he could win, if only he could avoid the humiliation of going to ask his friends for money, again.

It's his second-last coin. To think that before he got caught, he hid bundles of notes in mattresses, in books. It's inhuman, this downward spiral, Franz thinks.

The coin slips into the slot. Franz holds his breath. He presses the plastic button. On the screen, the symbols flash by.

Yes! He can't believe it! He's won!

The joy of all those tumbling coins! And in a week, his dole!

He's got enough to make it. He's happy. He leaves.

VIII

Armand has been for a walk in his new district. He's even bought a bike. It's 6 p.m. And he's on his way back to the apartment. He's happy, he's beginning to take control of his life here.

In the living room, Tobias is smoking a bubble pipe and tapping away on Otto's computer.

'Want some juice, Loulou?'

Armand nods; he won't refuse any experience; he's in a state of discovery.

Ten minutes go by. Armand has a sensation of self-awareness that is both simple and confused. Not like a sudden slap in the face, more of a hazy feeling of happiness; a synthetic calm. Relaxing with the same simplicity as when you dance. You breathe lightly. The first times you take it you don't have a powerful high. You feel happy without really knowing why. You don't get the too-violent effect of other narcotics. Before you abuse it, it's a subtle background state. You feel happy, talkative, and come to think of it, like you could fuck well, too.

The two of them chat, Tobias rolling his cigarettes, Armand taking bigger and bigger drags on the hookah, which looks like a holiday souvenir. What's he come here to do? Paint. Yes, that's what we need, painters. Above all, to live. What about girls? What sort do you like? Tall and blonde, a bit pale, ethereal. He likes it when they look lost in male company. Tobias knows some like that; he'll introduce him. Even better, they're not a pain in the arse like French girls.

Shall we do a bit more? Yeah, it's been an hour.

It could be ten minutes or two hours; you lose track. It's nice not worrying.

'There's bound to be a bit of speed in Otto's room. I'll go and look, we're pretty wrecked. A little bit will do. That's fine. No, don't use your money, that's disgusting. There are straws in the cupboard. Yes, cut it. Ah, that's better, this'll buck us up. Oh shit, the juice. I'm going to take some vitamins. They're better than Coke. They also take the taste away and you get the benefit of the calcium and magnesium. That's important. When you get high, you need to know how to keep in shape. I'll give you some cream for your hands. That's important too. Speeds dries your hands out. Here, have some vitamins. How much do you want? 1? 1.2? Yeah, one's enough. Here. I'm going to take a bit more. 1.1 should do it. It's not too much and you feel it more. I've been taking it for four years and I've never had a problem. Well yeah, I have, but that's from something else. What'll we do next? Let's go and see Chrissi; she has good speed. You got a bit of dough? We'll see, but we only need two grams. Ten euros each. We'll be sorted for the whole weekend. Chrissi's cool. She might give us a bit of free ketamine. She's fifty-five. She's a drug therapist. She looked after me, you know, when I wasn't well. I slept at her place and cooked for her. Risotto, soup – gloopy stuff like that. She likes that.'

Chrissi has a little ground-floor apartment. The big window looking on to the street is hidden behind curtains. The old druggie girls hide themselves away here. They know they can gossip without being spied on. It's a little world of recluses. They get high together, here or somewhere else, though they don't really like each other. There's not much laughter, the only thing being shared is drugs. It's a little community of loners, all of them seeking their own mind-numbing pleasure. Would they still be friends, if they had no drugs to share? But they do share, and you might mistake it for a real community.

There's sheeting on the floor in the living room. A few books, very few. Like in the homes of people who read out of boredom. There's also a desk; some scattered papers – that's the way of it – and a computer pumping out music. There's a guy sitting at it. He doesn't speak, he's selecting tracks.

Beyond that is the bedroom with a mattress on the wooden floor. Chrissi's lying there; it almost looks like she's asleep. It's the ketamine, Tobias says. Some clothes, a bed, Chrissi sleeping, that's it.

On the other side is the kitchen. That's where it happens. On top of the fridge, a mirror, a card and two heaps of white powder, speed and ketamine. On the worktop beside the sink are a large carafe of vitamins, three syringes in a glass and a phial of GHB. One by one, people help themselves at their own pace, on top of the fridge or beside the sink. Tobias is talking to Rémi. Their paths haven't crossed for several months. They used to party together a few years back, in the good old days. They fill each other in on people they no longer see. Since Rémi comes from Toulouse, they speak French. Sophie? Yeah, she's quit, she's got a kid. She's working and stuff. Marion? Give over, she's in Kottbusser Tor. That's a way of saying that she's gone to another level: heroin, crack, the Kottbusser Tor squats. Pierre? I heard he's gone back to Austria. Yeah, Martin's out of jail; he's being careful.

Standing in Chrissi's little kitchen, Armand feels he has entered a little world whose ways he hasn't mastered yet. He doesn't know how much to take. He's feeling his way. Sometimes he's a bit scared, but it passes, because he likes the state he gets into. He's speaks to Rémi.

It's odd, we're a bit limited. Chrissi gave us speed because we gave her juice. It's hard finding

GHB at the moment. David got caught. You can order on the internet, but that's risky and anyway you don't always have an address or a bank account. Lucy has some from time to time; we'd better call her next week if we don't run into her this weekend.

Hey, the guy at the computer's put on a great track. People start dancing. It's dark outside. Makes no difference, the curtains protect us. Chrissi's still asleep on her mattress. Rémi, Gando, Tobias and Armand throw themselves into the dancing in the living room. The bedroom door's open. Chrissi doesn't look like she's about to wake up. The guy at the computer smiles for the first time. He's a DJ or something. He's obsessed with his machines. He doesn't get as high as the rest of them. But from time to time he gets up from his chair to go and do a line in the kitchen. Because everyone's dancing, he gives them a smile. Maybe that was what he was waiting for after all.

Time passes; soon it's 5 a.m. Armand and Tobias are leaving.

'You coming? Let's go. To the Golden Gate. Hey, you look spaced out, Loulou. Me too. That's ketamine for you. Makes you elastic. Marshmallow legs. I can't walk any more; I'm folding. You seen my knees? They're bouncing. I get scared every time that I'll end up walking like this forever. Rémi's cool, isn't he? And Gando. Did you meet Gando? Everyone'll be at the Golden Gate. It's 5 o'clock, it's cool, we'll arrive at the right time. You'll see, it's nothing but mates. Party people. No little Frenchies. You're going to be a big hit with your pretty face. There are loads of girls. And guys for me too. Small, bearded, a bit muscly. Yeah, I need to feel their strength. That's what I really like, you know. I want them to take me like a whore. Rémi used to say that all the time. In French. No one understood him. In the middle of the dance floor he'd shout it out. "Take me like a whore! Take me like a whore!" He's not gay, it just made him laugh. You hungry? I think I am. I dunno. You want to go to McDonald's? No, you're right. Let's see after. Anyway, there's a Burger King beside the Golden Gate. At worst, we can go out and get something. A Whopper or something.'

Rémi doesn't go out any more, so he's not coming. Gando's in no state to go anywhere. Chrissi's asleep. They say goodbye. The guy at the computer has stopped smiling.

It was great; we've got to do it again. Call Chrissi, she's got my email.

There are very few people in the underground now. Some revellers, the odd worker, some tramps. Armand and Tobias take some GHB on the platform. That means taking out the Coke, the phial of juice, and most important, the syringe. Armand looks like he knows the ropes by now. He's no longer worrying about discovering who he is. He's walking around, his spirit free and his heart numb. He feels that at last he's living a little more intensely. He's discovering the side of existence that seems independent of Time. It's 5.30 a.m., they're high but beginning to come down – they've been like that for eighteen hours but nothing can stop their bodies. It's time to go and meet people. Have some fun.

'So, we take the U2 to Alexanderplatz. Then change – there's a McDonald's in the station, we can get a cheeseburger – then U8 to Jannowitzbrücke. The Golden Gate's right by the exit from the underground. Under the bridge, you'll see. Yeah, a cheeseburger would be great. I should have enough.'

'How do you pronounce the name of the station?'

'Jannowitzbrücke'

'Yanno–'

'Yes.'

'Veets–'

'Yes.'

'Broo-keh. That's funny, broo-keh separate from the rest. Wait, let me try. Yannoleetsbookeh. No, sorry, Yannovitzbroovkeh. Hey, I've got it. Jannowitzbrücke. Will you help me learn some German? If I'm going to stay here, I need to be able to speak. Speaking matters. You can say things to yourself and try to understand others. And instructions. When it comes to language it's not always straightforward. You get closer to people's thoughts. Course, they need to express themselves. Yes, that's it, they need to express themselves. It's never enough just hearing what they tell us. When I'm painting, I'm thinking about certain things, but what am I saying deep down? I don't know, maybe I should be trying to write them down. It's not easy to give all that you have, to strip yourself bare, as they say. You owe it to yourself to be sincere. Simple and sincere. Like the greats. The rest, the minor talents, lie, and in order to be believed they dress up what they say in false complexity. They count on our loss. Illusion through loss. It works, you know. And people often speak to each other like that. Little complications invented so as not to reveal too much. Maybe they think like that, I dunno. They can talk about insignificant stuff – I don't mean the little stuff of everyday poetry, no really, I mean the kind of stuff that has no meaning because it's empty – oh yeah, they can talk about that for hours. Empty heads. That's what it must be, empty heads. Or full of formaldehyde.'

It's a strange journey for Armand. As he's talking, he goes up to objects on the underground. The seats in the carriages are not the same colour, there's no turnstile, there's one platform for both directions, the train comes in from the right, all these things which are different from what he knows give him a feeling of huge freedom.

They change at Alexanderplatz; long corridors and empty doorways. Neon reflections shine on the marbled floor. You could walk on it barefoot. Some bad food smells, a staircase and then another platform. Armand flexes then folds his identity card. In the middle, a fat white line to share.

'Stop halfway. I'll have the rest.'

Armand obeys; he slowly registers the smell of the Polish dumplings; that smell will lodge itself in the back of his throat every day and for so long that it will never leave him. These are his first experiences with amphetamines, which he'll cherish. Speed is strong, it attacks the nostrils, you have to be prepared for it.

'It doesn't have an anaesthetic side to it like cocaine, but don't worry, it won't last long. That feeling that the powder is going off in your head like a rocket. In two minutes, you'll be as good as new, able to dance for days. You don't need to keep taking it every twenty minutes, you'll see, if it's good, one fix and you're sorted for four hours. Well, only as long as you don't do something dumb with the juice. Take my advice, if you feel the juice is taking you over, a good line of speed and it'll be gone, it'll put your feet back on the ground. But stay off the booze, I'm not kidding, Loulou, not even one beer. And if you've had too much, and you're flailing around and your muscles are moving on their own, a nice line of speed will bring you back down.'

The Golden Gate

Entry is through a small metal door. The bearded bouncer is intimidating – but he hugs Tobias, gently. He's introduced to Armand in German.

'*Hallo, ich bin Armand. Ich komme aus Paris. Alles gut*?' – the only sentence he has mastered.

'*Klar*!'

On the right beyond the cash desk, there's what looks like a little garden with lots of sofas and armchairs. It's not daylight yet; there aren't many people outside. The club itself is on the left of the cash desk under a U-Bahn bridge. The corridor is dark and the music pounding. You go down some stairs, then there's the cloakroom, a bar at the back, armchairs if you fancy a break. It's festive, steamy, exists beyond time.

Another room. Everyone's dancing, facing towards the DJ. The atmosphere seems serious, the dancers' movements repetitive and jerky. This is minimalist dancing, not like in Paris's few techno clubs. The boys are not pawing the girls; though everyone's high, there's a kind of restraint. You go all out to get high, you leave yourself, but to be respected by others, you have to behave properly. Armand catches on fast, he grasps the customs.

The toilets are upstairs. People go in singly, in couples, even in fives.

Hours go by, it gets light outside. Neon lights, sweat. *Druffis* wander about, disorientated. A taste of GHB in your mouth. Talk is sporadic – you OK? – Tell me your name again – yes, I'm from Paris, I came here to paint – you want something? – Give me a kiss.

In a cubicle in the bogs. There's filth on the floor. Armand has his arms round a girl he doesn't know. He gives her some juice. She kneels down, unbuttons his trousers, briefly slides his cock between her lips and then stands up. They're going to dance. Already he's almost forgotten her. He won't bump into her again. Like everyone else, he has picked up an empty beer bottle that had been left against a wall. In the toilets he rinses it out and fills it with water; to rehydrate himself, and help the juice go down. After a few hours, he seems used to it. But he's new to this all the same. Other people can tell easily, they've never seen his face before. It's a small world where everyone ends up knowing everyone. Whether they say hello or not, you know the people dancing beside you. That's where the *Drogensolidarität* comes from. A whole recreational community that gets high together, among fellow initiates. Some people are in fancy dress, suspender belts and lace basques; confetti gets thrown in the air, and there are glitter balls too. The joys are synthetic and outsized. It instantly feels like a new facet of existence. The feeling of living more intensely, the pride – perverse and displaced – that gives.

Armand and Tobias meet up again. They dance side by side. They haven't seen each other for about an hour. They are moving to an odd track, tribal voices, broken rhythms.

'Armand, I've got to tell you. I'm HIV-positive.'

Armand stops dancing. Tobias takes his hand.

'Come on, fuck it, let's dance.'

There's something strange about the idea of this evening going on forever. Outside it's broad daylight. They can't see it, they're dancing in a little club that has no windows.

'I saw you with a girl a while ago. I didn't think she was your type.'

'Oh, it wasn't like that. She's nice, kind of lost.'

'Yeah, I've seen her before. She gets high on the juice too. What's her name?'

'I forget. She's nice. Shall we go out for a fag?'

In the little garden, dozens of people are sitting in the armchairs. Sunglasses or troubled expressions. They're smoking cigarettes and joints. You can hardly hear the music. You can talk here, and take a bit of a rest.

'You still got the bottle I gave you?'

'Yeah.'

'You got much left?'

'Half.'

'Ten mil each. Plus the twenty I left outside. That's good, we've got enough for the Berghain. You'll see, there's nothing better than the Pano on a Sunday. Everyone'll be there for sure. I'll introduce you. You'll be a star.'

A few joints, several fixes of GHB. Tobias talks a lot, in the toilets, as he prepares the drugs. There are always other people sharing the cubicles with them. The conversations are disjointed, often funny and meaningless.

They hang around for a while.

Outside, the daylight blinds them. It's funny how calm it is, when you cross Holzmarktstrasse to get to the S-Bahn station.

'Shit, I forgot to pick up the juice. Wait for me, I'll be right back.'

Like everywhere in this city, the streets are huge. Waiting on the other side of the street, Armand feels good. He watches the regular flow of traffic. He's smiling. He's discovering the narcotic effect of GHB, of existing outside time.

'It's OK, I got it. One stop and we're there. We'll take the juice inside. You've got to look in shape for the bouncers. Just like before. Hide your bottle, syringe and speed in your pants. They search really thoroughly at the Pano. There are approved dealers, you see. And you mustn't mention the juice too much. People don't like that. A year or two ago they had a lot of problems. The ambulances were turning up every weekend because people didn't know how to take it; they were boozing and everything. Don't tell anyone that you're taking G. It's good though, isn't it?'

'Fuck yeah.'

IX

Tobias recognises the guy who's coming out of the S-Bahn at the same time as them. It's Franz. He's going to the Panorama too. They join up. They can go together, Armand, Franz and Tobias. Another regular Sunday at the Berghain.

X

Armand goes home from the Berghain alone. It must be thirty hours since he slept. He remembers Sigrid offering him her body in the toilets at the Panorama. He also remembers the brunette at the Golden Gate.

He doesn't feel tired or hungry. He's only going home because the evening has gone on long enough. He thinks of a line in a book by David Goodis, which he savours sometimes, *after a while it gets so bad that you want to stop the whole business.* The evening was starting to turn sour, Armand could feel it turning, that all he would end up with was a great, jaundiced feeling of melancholy and he had to go, go home to bed.

It's dark outside. It could have been daylight and Armand wouldn't have been surprised. He hasn't just stepped outside Habit, but also Time, though it's hard to know whether Time is friend or foe. He's humming that song: *Time won't let us stop.*

He's not in a hurry. The idea of taking the underground, of finding himself sitting opposite people he can't escape causes him real anxiety. He prefers the streets, drifting along as a pedestrian; you pass others by and they can't look at you for very long. They're following their own route, going who knows where. There are none of those underground-carriage faces judging you.

Armand has always liked the anonymity of big cities. In Paris he thought he had lost it at one point because he hung around the same districts, frequented the same bars. Here there's not much risk of running into someone he knows; it's the freedom of being abroad.

He doesn't really know which way to go. The tower in Alexanderplatz is a good landmark. Wherever you are in Berlin, you can pick it out on the skyline. He walks towards the tower, so straight and so real that for a moment he has no sense of never having trod these pavements before. The wind is blowing. It isn't cold; it's a mild autumn.

Occasionally he crosses streets bordered by

unlit waste ground. In the distance, he can see a petrol station, but he doesn't come across any other pedestrians or cars. It feels like an industrial zone in the middle of the city. The discreet charm of industry.

Armand walks on towards the television tower. He can feel the little bottle of GHB in his pocket. He might be home within the hour.

XI

Tobias and Franz are looking for people to keep partying with. When they emerged from the Berghain as it was closing, Armand had gone. They hung around, waiting for the last people to leave. Someone was bound to organise an after.

Why would they stop? They aren't hungry or tired.

You find the world's dodgiest characters at these afters in apartments, so they always leave you with the sort of bitter taste that prickles your tongue, or stings your cheeks. They are like the smoke from badly tamped pipes.

They wound up at the place of some guy they knew vaguely, talking about nothing much.

They left.

Now they're hungry. They aren't that far from Otto's. He'll have bacon. Off they go.

XII

There were too many amphetamines still clogging his arteries, so Armand hasn't slept well. Interrupted, troubled sleep, the sleep of pure exhaustion, which struggles with the narcotics that still intermittently trouble your guts.

When he got up, a cigarette in his mouth, he was touched to see Tobias and Franz sleeping like children on the living room sofa. Because they were still dressed, there couldn't have been anything sexual in it.

Otto is up too. He shares some tea with Armand at the breakfast bar, a few metres from the sofa. They talk softly, indistinctly almost, so as not to wake them.

Armand mentions Sigrid. Otto smiles. Next time, maybe he'll come along too.

XIII

Armand has found a watering hole he likes near the apartment. He goes there every day to work on his drawings, after sharing some bacon and scrambled eggs with his flatmates.

He likes the route he takes. Schönhauser Allee as far as Eberswalderstrasse, then Kastanienallee. The girls are prettier on Kastanienallee. Some streets are like that, as though you can almost smell their perfume. Armand likes to walk these streets, catch people's eye, the hint of a smile in a flicker of an eyelid.

He's used to his route. He already knows the shop windows. The hairdresser's with the table football, the brown leather bike saddles made by Brooks, which make him drool but are much too expensive for him.

So first there are these shops, and then Kastanienallee and its blondes, the kebab shop on the corner, the clothes shop with dozens of T-shirts with Bolshevik designs hanging up outside.

Finally he reaches his bar. It's a small room with green seats; it looks like a Russian living room. The light is beige, very different from the terrible white light from those economy lightbulbs that dazzle your eyes.

There's a little marble table on the mezzanine, the only one where you can smoke. Armand sits there. The waitress recognises him. He gives his order in German the way Tobias has taught him.

'*Hallo, ein Espresso, ein Aschenbecher und ein Chococroissant, bitte.*'

He's proud of this sentence, of being able to utter it, and in German if you please. The waitress smiles at him. She thinks it's cute, this French accent you could cut with a knife. She comes back shortly with a glass ashtray, a coffee and a chocolate croissant. She puts them on the table and slips in a simple '*et voilà*' in French, with that accent that German girls have, tender and sensual.

The waitress is pretty. Brunette, quite tall. She's sweet, best of all. It would be good to rest his head in the small of her back or between her breasts, on that firm, delicate skin. She has a calm sensuality that Armand likes in women. He can almost feel the skin of her belly, her thighs, her back, a few beauty spots. Her whole body sums up what Armand misses, the privations of a single man; care and caresses. She seems to be inviting him, smiling at him. Something happens between them when she comes to his table, carrying the little metal tray. It's not just Armand who feels it; it's mutual.

She puts down the ashtray, coffee and chocolate croissant.

'*Et voilà…*'

Armand feels himself melt. They look at each other for a moment, sadly, as though inevitably aware it is not to be. She goes back to her work. Armand is drawing at the little marble table.

An hour later, they say goodbye in the way that a customer says goodbye to a waitress. Armand goes home; he doesn't look at the blonde girls on Kastanienallee.

XIV

Tobias and Franz are in the S-Bahn, the S41, which encircles the city like a little yellow-gold chain. It's 2 p.m., morning rush hour for the out-of-sync people.

Tobias lost his phone the previous week. He and Franz are going to see that guy Stein; Tobias lent another phone to him a few months back.

The S-Bahn stops at the next station. A couple of guys in trainers and unfashionable anoraks are chatting on the platform. When the doors open, they split up and each of them boards through a different carriage door.

Berlin has plain-clothes ticket inspectors. Since there's no turnstile to jump, they check tickets on the trains, working their way through the carriage from one end to the other. They don't let you off, as they're paid on commission. They're often former fraudsters; it's a rehabilitation scheme. You have to pay forty euros on the spot, in cash or with a bank card, otherwise you're off to the police station and all that hassle.

Franz and Tobias are on the lookout; they don't have a ticket and they can't afford forty euros.

When they spotted the two guys on the platform at Landsberger Allee, they calmly got off. They'll go on foot; it's safer. Stein's place isn't far.

There's an element of professionalism in their fraud. They are attentive; they couldn't have missed those two wolves.

They've arrived outside Stein's place. This is definitely it, Tobias remembers it. They don't have the entry code for his building.

There's no one they can call. Tobias doesn't have a phone any more, and Franz sold his ages ago. In any case, they wouldn't know what number to call. They wait outside the block for someone to go in or come out. Franz rolls a cigarette.

A guy goes in and they follow him. They knock

on Stein's door. A Turkish woman opens it. Stein moved a month ago; she doesn't know how to find him.

'You're not the first people to come looking for him. I don't know who this Stein is, but he doesn't seem right to me. He left the apartment in a terrible state.'

Tobias and Franz take the S-Bahn home, the S42, which loops the city in the opposite direction. They'll get something to eat at Otto's.

XV

Armand bought a bike at the Gorlitzer Park flea market. It's an old racer. The frame is grey; the handlebars, like rams horns, are wrapped in white tape. His hands grip them, and the tips of his shoes stick in the metal spikes on the pedals.

Armand has a feeling of security when he gets on his bike – he can't slip off it, his slick tyres seem to float over the road surface, he's following a clear route, making a necessary journey.

He rides his bike for several hours a day, going wherever his fancy takes him. He chooses streets he likes, follows them for a bit, then turns off. He gets lost, rides among the cars, among men, going slowly or quickly. It's a game. He loses his way and finds it again without ever asking for directions.

On his bike, he feels alone with the city; he talks to it, touches it. It's an enormous pleasure when he's lost and pedalling down streets where he doesn't recognise anything, to find his way back, to realise exactly where he is thanks to a junction, a bar, an underground station or whatever. He knows at that moment that he's beginning to master this city, that he has seduced it, that he holds all the cards and can penetrate the very depths of its being.

He's won the battle. He hangs around for a bit on the streets or in a bar, snug in this tarmac cradle that belongs to him, this city where he's no longer just a tourist.

As he rides, he practises pronouncing place-names. Schlesisches Tor, Schlesisches Tor. He stumbles over the language, tries again. He wants to know this city in the same way as knowing a girl. To feel her, taste her, and later remember the smell of her skin.

He hangs around on a café terrace on Oranienstrasse. He reads a bit, then goes back to his beer, rolls a cigarette and smokes it as he looks around.

He knows the way home. When he's ready, he'll go back. He'll abandon the streets and the women passing by, return to his bed and wait for tomorrow.

PART THREE

Winter

1

When he wakes, his jaw hurts. He stretches in his warm bed; the sheets are [illegible]. He glances at the window, or rather, the sky, through the pane. It's winter. It's so cold outside.

The sky is mocking him. There is no [illegible], like a big grey cloche over the city. You can't see the sun or clouds, only this asphalt-coloured blanket, a sheet stretched between people and the heavens, a sheet that is holding back all hope. This dome of suffering.

Armand half-sits. He lights his first cigarette of the day. The cloud drifts towards the [illegible] panes; he watches it rise to the ceiling [illegible] dreams. The grey smoke of a [illegible] alone, [illegible] and watching, slowly losing its [illegible]. The smoke will coat the walls of the [illegible] bedroom, the colour of all the hours spent waiting in vain for life to blossom.

It's four months today since [illegible].

He gets up. A new day begins.

I

When he wakes, his jaw hurts. He stretches out in his warm bed; the sheets are clammy. He glances at the window, or rather the sky, through the pane. It's winter. It's so cold outside.

The sky is mocking him. There *is* no sky. It's like a big grey cloche over the city. You can't see the sun or clouds, only this asphalt-coloured blanket, a sheet stretched between people and the heavens, a sheet that is holding back all hope. The dome of suffering.

Armand half-sits. He lights his first cigarette of the day. The cloud drifts upwards and disperses; he watches it rise to the ceiling like broken dreams. The grey smoke of a man alone, smoking and watching, slowly losing its form in the room. The smoke will coat the walls in the yellow of boredom, the colour of all the hours spent watching in vain for life to blossom.

It's four months today since Armand arrived.

He gets up. A new day begins.

II

For several weeks, the street has lost its old appeal. Its heart is frozen, its surface covered in snow. They shovel the snow up in some places, on the roads, in front of shops, which then turn to mud, leaving a thin layer that your shoes slip on.

No one panics; people here are used to putting on boots, taking a shovel to clear their doorways. It's as though a parallel life is activated: bikes and tables outside cafés are put away, hats and tights are taken out, daylight becomes unfamiliar, there are invitations to people's flats for soup or a cup of tea. The out-of-sync people change their rhythm, too; it's dark at 4 p.m., so it's best to try not to get up too late. But it's a time of celebration, the clubs are never busier than at these times, when everyone is seeking a bit of warmth.

Armand has got used to this life. He feels like he belongs to this scene. For the first time in his life, he feels as though he knows where his generation is at. He can already picture himself telling his children about the adventures and mistakes of his youth. Because even if Armand is living it fully and could live no other way at this point, he cannot imagine staying ten years, eventually dying beneath a glitter ball.

He doesn't do drugs because he's disgusted at life; it's maybe more out of a love of life, since his sensations, his loves, his one-night stands, his joys and his pains are all so much more intense. It's an adventure he's instigated; it's no less noble or real for that. The locations and the substances don't matter, because those feelings are powerfully present within him.

That is the essential difference between Armand and Tobias; for Armand, these are extraordinary sensations and for Tobias they are normal.

Tobias had to leave Otto's place. Five months is a long time to sleep on the same sofa. He moved in with Franz, at the apartment he's been lent. They did a deal; Tobias pays the electricity and gets the second bedroom. It's in Neukölln, the last Turkish district in the south of the city.

III

There's this girl, Sarah, that Armand snogs every Sunday at the Panorama. He's never had sex with her in the toilets – that's not her style. Sarah doesn't do drugs. But she's there every week, dancing with the rest of them. Sarah's a graphic designer; just about everyone here is. She comes on her own, without friends or drugs; she just comes, since she feels at ease with herself.

This evening, Armand has arranged to meet Sarah for a drink, away from the Berghain, at Kottbusser Tor. He's excited at the thought of seeing her, but a little anxious too. It feels a bit like he's falling for her.

It's the first time this has happened since he arrived; he sleeps with two, three, four, even five girls a week. He's confident, everyone's high, and it's easy, direct, brutal sex in the toilet cubicles; standing up, unprotected, a few thrusts of the pelvis as an intermission between dances. The girl pulls her knickers up and they leave the toilets without kissing. Most of the time, he can hardly remember them; they are just hazy encounters with anonymous girls.

But this one's different. He's going to meet Sarah to have a drink and talk. Normally, he turns down this sort of invitation, he's not keen on seeing them again, the Berghain girls; he's gone down on them in the toilet cubicles, he's taken them from behind, without restraint, and that's quite enough. But this time something is impelling him. Perhaps Sarah is the one after all.

They meet outside the underground. It's snowing. Sarah isn't that pretty to be honest; not that great a body either, not the sort he'd dream about. And yet he desires her more than any other, because every time they've kissed, there's been electricity between them, a dark prickle of desire.

They kiss on the cheek like friends. They walk for a bit. Let's go in here, this bar's quite trendy.

They have a few beers. Armand tells some stories that make her laugh. He feels strong when he's talking to her; she listens to him wide-eyed; Armand's reflection sparkles at the edge of her pupils. When he runs out of things to say, he kisses her. He feels her melt, feels her body yielding to him entirely after a kiss.

They go to her place.

He begins undressing her on the stairs. They're in a hurry. She's laughing. Armand slips his hand up her skirt while she's opening the door. He feels her little thighs tremble, her slit open. They throw themselves on the bed; they get rid of their clothes as best they can, kiss again, lick each other, or rather taste each other, and fuck, eagerly.

When he takes her, Armand understands why he wanted to see her again. She looks like his ex,

Emma, the only one he loved. That's not apparent from her features or the shape of her breasts. No, it's deeper than that. She has the same taste, her skin, her body has the same smell, the same flavour.

He realises this as he comes, violently, in Sarah.

IV

The apartment seems spacious, but Tobias and Armand only ever see the crummy little kitchen. That's where Fritz receives them.

Fritz is Swiss. He claims he's an artist. He puts up the kind of installation you see everywhere, piles of wood or polystyrene.

They talk a bit to be polite, to try to make it a bit less uncivil, but all three of them know that that's not why they're there.

After a while, Fritz says what they've been waiting to hear: 'How much do you want?'

Fritz supplies small nightclub dealers. His speed is strong; he sells at a ludicrous price, around three euros a gram, because he shifts it in quantity.

Tobias and Armand buy as much as they can; they spend all the money they have left. It won't be a wasted investment; speed sells fast in club toilets, and for more than three times what they paid.

When they go back to Armand's place, it's always the same routine; they divide up their treasure.

Armand enjoys this activity, filling the little bags with a gram – always a little less, business is business – using his electronic scales. The calculations are looking good. We spent sixty euros; we'll earn 240 and three grams left over for us. It's going to be a good weekend, yeah, it's going to be a good one. Club tickets, juice, cigarettes and sandwiches, they can pay for the lot.

They put the speed in the fridge to keep it fresh. Yeah, it's going to be a good one.

V

Juli is ten. She's long understood what kind of a man her father is. She realises that she can never rely on him, that he can't cope with other people any more than with himself.

Franz is elegant; something about his appearance would never make you suspect he leads the life he does. But Juli is too familiar with his unwillingness to meet your eye, his look of shame, to be taken in. She knows that if he comes to see them – her and her mother, Juli and Martha Krüll, the pastor's granddaughter and daughter – it's because he's hungry and has lost everything, because he always ends up losing everything.

When Franz knocks on the door, they know it's him even before they open. The hours he keeps are like no one else's, not the postman, not Mum's friends.

Martha always gets a bit emotional when Franz visits. It doesn't matter what state he's in, she's always glad to see him. And perhaps he'll have changed, who knows? It's been so long since he last came.

Juli doesn't want to hear anything about him. She doesn't want him to kiss her, to say that she's got bigger, or call her his girl. She doesn't want a loser for a father. She persists in not believing him. She knows that Mum will lend him money; she knows they won't see him again for several weeks, until the next time. She has the impression of a swindle being committed against her. She doesn't want him to ask her how things are at school. She can manage perfectly well without him. As soon as he's around, there are complications. Mum says she has a migraine, she shuts herself away in her room and cries; she takes her medicine to sleep, which makes her a different person. Everything was going fine, but he had to come back. After he's been, the house, where she plays and laughs, becomes a temple of damaged nerves.

Today when Franz came, Juli, his own daughter, told him that she didn't want to see him again. She gave him her savings – twenty-five euros – and asked him to go.

VI

Tobias has invited Armand to dinner at his and Franz's place.

It's in a part of Neukölln that Armand doesn't know, far to the south, a long way from Kreuzberg and the Turkish market. Although he looked at a map before he left, when he comes out of the S-Bahn, he gets lost. The avenues are big and lonely, devoid of people, streets that seem to have given up the ghost. No shops or pedestrians, just a few faded signs, and dirty snow as far as the eye can see.

Armand lights a cigarette, a reflex action, because he's alone and cold, and doesn't know which way to go. Choosing a direction at random isn't an easy task. These streets look nothing like the map; they are much less straight, much bigger, and impossible to follow with your index finger. It had seemed easy: left and then second right when you come out of the underground. But it turns out there are lots of underground exits. There are lots and Armand is lost.

There's a guy over there. A guy crossing the road. Armand runs over to him. He's a Turk; he speaks German but no English. At times like this, Armand feels very foreign, as though the whole city is reproaching him for not making enough of an effort. He stammers three sentences in German; he doesn't know how to get to an address he's been given. It's not the first time he's got lost, of course, but this time the feeling of anxiety has crept up on him; a sharp sensation catches his stomach, like when he arrived at holiday camp as a boy. He'd lost his bearings, he was no longer sure of who he was. He didn't know where he'd sleep that night. It was strange, being away from home. He felt terribly alone.

The guy who was crossing the street shows him the way with a few gestures. And off Armand goes. It's the right street; he's there, he's found Franz's place.

Tobias and Franz are sitting in the kitchen. They're peeling vegetables. On a corner of the table, a little bottle of GHB, a syringe and a big carafe of fizzy vitamins seem to be waiting for someone to pick them up. It makes a strange sight, this still life, the fresh vegetable peelings, as though still wet with morning dew, and the little drugs kit.

'Come and sit down, Armand. Take that chair there. Fix yourself some juice, Loulou. You hungry?'

Since they have known each other, Tobias has been playing this role for Armand, looking after him, trying to give him what he thinks is best. He makes him sit down, get a bit high, then eat. These maternal concerns may be misplaced but they are terribly sincere. This is what he knows best, for the body and soul.

Armand does as he's told. He has already mastered the routine. A mouthful of vitamins. The GHB goes into the syringe – 0.8 to start with, that's not too bad. In his mouth he mixes it with the vitamins. He swallows it all and then has another drink to take the taste away. He has learned to recognise this taste; he would know it anywhere. He realises exactly what he's doing, what substance he's dealing with. It's a drug he's familiar with now, since he's taken it almost every day for several months. As an initiate, he has entered their little circle. When he thinks about it, Armand feels a little misplaced pride. He's already known as G-star in the toilets at the Panorama. He's proud he's mastered how to use it. He believes he has chosen the road he's on with his accidental companions.

So he had his fix almost as soon as he got to Franz's, a fix that had his name on it – as though he had made it entirely himself. He's playing the part of a drug addict as some people play the role of a café waiter: his changing appearance, the aesthetic of his pose, the cult of the formal, precise poetry of those who live for their pleasures, for unknown sensations. It's a goal of existence, the lost search for narcotic pleasures. Are they not all seeking pleasure? What else is there to guide our lives? For Armand, it's that simple, he has never before experienced such intense pleasure. Or maybe he did when he was in love with Emma. But he lost her. He's trying something else, that's all. There is no meaning. So live for what you love. At one point it was Emma, now it's GHB. He's throwing himself into it body and soul. The question for him is not whether it's appropriate. It suits him; it's as simple as that. Perhaps it's temporary, perhaps not. For the moment, it's like playing the café waiter.

They had something to eat and then Astrid arrived. She's a friend of Tobias's and has come to cut their hair. That's her job; she's brought a little metal case with all her kit in it.

They talk and take drugs at the little kitchen table. There's music. They have fun in a laid-back way.

Astrid is twenty-five. She works in a salon in the west, somewhere quite posh. She's brunette, quite pretty, that sort of cute beauty that doesn't hit you over the head; she has a way of looking at you, of moving and smiling, that makes her charming, almost touching. She has little red cheeks and bobbed hair; she'd know how to look after you, in a bed or in a chair, with tenderness and attention. Her skin probably doesn't taste incredible, but she's sweet for sure, certainly enough to take her seriously. Hers is not the sort of beauty that promises great adventures, but a sincere, agreeable life.

Franz watches her as she talks; she laughs at his jokes. He'd like to know her, to sample peace and the balm of simple affection. She likes cutting hair, she knows what she's doing .

They get started. Franz goes and wets his hair,

and Tobias puts a chair in front of the mirror in the bedroom.

When she touches Franz's head, she has a way of taking hold of locks of hair, in three fingers, from the roots to the tips, to gauge how long they are. It's a graceful, professional gesture, of the utmost gentleness.

Franz, sitting in the chair, watches her in the mirror. She's standing behind him, her eyes focused on his hair. From time to time, they exchange glances in the mirror; she gives a quick smile then gets back to work. It's been a long time since anyone bothered about Franz like this, with attention and gentleness.

She's doing him a favour, as a friend, though just a few hours before, they hadn't met. She moves closer to him, leans her stomach against the chair, from time to time one of her breasts brushes against Franz's head. It's troublingly intimate, almost like a dance; him, sitting in front of the mirror and her, standing at his back. He can feel her breathing and almost nestling against him. He looks at her in the mirror and thinks she's beautiful.

The haircut is over, they move apart. The locks of dead hair are strewn over the floor like privileged witnesses of this intimacy. Now it's

Armand's turn and then Tobias's, but they won't be suitors, they won't dance with her. She'll cut their hair and that's all.

They stay in the apartment a while longer, floating to the rhythm of the music and the drugs, then happily set off for the Golden Gate, sporting their brand-new haircuts.

PART FOUR

‘The Promised Land Just Got Further Away’

I

A few weeks have gone by. Armand is in his room, writing in his little grey notebook:

News from Tobias at last. Not very joyful but reassuring all the same (I thought he was dead). He's in jail, at least till the twenty-third. Overdose in the underground + €2,000 worth of gear on him. He says he found it; I think Fritz probably gave it to him because he wanted to give up – his mate's paralysed (he jumped out of a window on acid). His letter's a bit confused. That's all I have. Since Franz asked, I told him Tobias was in Paris; feel a bit bad about lying to him (we searched everywhere for him together, hoping he hadn't killed himself – I think that's what Franz was thinking too). I'd like to go and see him; he doesn't want visitors, doesn't give the address. I'd like to be able to do something.

This sentence at the end of the letter: 'prison is hell'.

It's the misfortune he lacked. Something of fate which has persecuted him; this feeling that in addition it is persecuting a small boy. I hope he knows at least that he can count on me. I feel as though I owe him something, that I owe it to him to help as much as I can. For the moment, there's nothing I can do; but he is going to need me.

I'm holding myself back, as though I couldn't let the sadness take hold of my body, for fear I would not recover.

II

Armand is in a photo booth, eyes wide open, looking into the darkness of the lens. There are four dazzling flashes in succession. He's wearing a red cap and smoking. He gets up, opens the curtain and waits in the street by the machine for the strip of pictures. The photos drop. He looks at them, gives a little laugh and puts them in his coat. He goes off. The pavements on Kastanienallee are covered in brown snow.

Armand is on the escalator in a shopping centre. He's listening to music on his headphones. His head is moving in rhythm, making jerky neck movements. He steps off and heads for the supermarket. He has a list in his hand. He looks lost.

In his room, Armand opens two little plastic sachets. He prepares a line of ketamine, then one of speed, on the mirror. He pops the earphones of his MP3 player in and does both lines. He paints for a while, on a board on the floor. But his creative efforts tire him. He dances, alone, attached to the cord of his MP3 player, as though he wanted to do something unproductive.

Armand arrives at the entrance to the Berghain. He looks a bit the worse for wear, as though sadness had slightly altered his features. The bouncer recognises him; he senses that Armand has lost his innocence. He'd like to say to him simply, *hey, son, go home. You can't pull that hard or the rope will snap. It's Sunday, it's cold but the weather is nice. Go home, son, you're better than this.* But he doesn't say anything; it's his job to see them all cross his threshold, one after the other.

Armand goes in. Hidden in his pants, he has a bottle of GHB, some speed and ketamine.

III

Astrid moved in with Franz.

They bicker a bit, laugh and kiss. He likes to feel

her body wriggle against his. They approach each other then separate, circle each other as though they wanted to combine their savours.

Astrid has three days off work, so they don't get out of bed. They fall asleep sometimes, kiss, watch TV series on Astrid's computer. They make love, out of reach, between two siestas. It's their lovers' hideaway as a means to discovery; they don't get up unless they have to, to have a pee or get a glass of water. It feels so natural, protected there, smoking, eating, talking and caressing each other under the quilt. The world is so cold. They're shutting themselves away and keeping each other warm. Just the two of them, outside time.

This burgeoning love, still completely unconstrained, is a rare happiness; spending hours on end together doing nothing, the best thing they've ever known. In a few hours, it'll be time to face the world again, Astrid will go to work and Franz will do what Franz does; they'll be separated, so best make the most of it, rest your head on her belly and wait, at peace.

IV

Armand, alone with his notebook:

Haven't managed to keep off them this week. Yesterday, open air; MDMA, GHB and speed. Need to cut myself off from the druffis *who will never do me any good.*

Some news from Tobias by text. Asking me to do strange things, such as getting out all the breakfast things on the kitchen table. I can't get rid of the idea that it's a trap. But I should trust him.

There's a girl who's pretty and interesting, though probably unpleasant, who I see on Kastanienallee. Black coat.

Saw her twenty minutes later, carrying a cardboard tube; I think there may be something.

I've begun; I've got the plan, the idea, everything I need in fact, but I don't like it, I'm not painting well. And yet I'm applying myself seriously. Until it's rejected, I can't identify exactly what's wrong with the last series. If it were accepted, would I stop painting? I don't think so, but I'd continue doing the same shit.

Watched a film by M on the internet a few times; pretty great and exemplifies in a way what I'm experiencing here. I lack images; it did me good to see some again; should I be taking photos, making films? It wouldn't come instinctively to me; but I like watching them. I like taking advantage of other people's.

Gave myself some more tattoos (that makes five); dots on my hand, an A on my foot. Compared to the three others, of course, they're not up to much but these new ones have a kind of homemade charm, from the knowledge that I did them myself, with a needle and India ink.

Dany is celebrating his first year on drugs at the fusion festival.

Needle plus joint (face numb).

Pretty blonde waitress at the Haliflor.

Want to get my soul back. I've done myself enough harm.

Deep disgust for GHB; remember this state if I'm tempted to start taking too much again.

Need something else – refocus myself on painting (because I think that that, after all, is the best thing life can offer me), stop trying to treat my suffering with poison; that suffering makes me paint. I don't want to lose that. Not to mention the fact I'm wrecking my brain; a pianist chopping off his own fingers.

I think about my childhood, my adolescence (am I an adult?). I've got a nasty taste in my mouth.

Fortunately words get me out of that state.

There's something too confining about life. I aspire to more than life (this passion, drugs, creation).

Boredom and sadness, at the root of it all?

Going down, the desire for aphorisms. They seem to sound good. Reread tomorrow.

I smoke cigarettes one after the other and never grow tired of them.

I always have to be consuming something.

I've partied; I don't feel dirty though; no, it was a necessary purge.

Sleep soundly tonight, and tomorrow, painting.

I love this city, and this life.

Otto and Claudia have gone to do some work in northern Germany. Armand is alone in the apartment.

I don't go out, I observe.

I look at my body, the neighbours, the kitchen walls. I'm home alone; not talking. It's going pretty well, I think about my little problems, do the washing-up, take baths. I listen to music, the lights are on. I walk about as much as I can. I need to work my muscles before they disappear.

Sometimes I do a few push-ups.

I don't really think about it, this is my life now. I have rituals. Perhaps they save me, they're always the same.

But sometimes the strangeness of my life jumps out at me like some unpleasant bug.

Generally this happens when I switch off the light or the music; those artificial presences no longer protect me and I dream, sadly, about my loneliness, the void that surrounds me and is devouring me. Most of the time, though, I'm not aware of this void; it floats around me like a friend, the inoffensive companion of my pain.

The days fly past without me remembering them. They're too similar to tell them apart.

It's been several days since I last washed. My skin is a bit sticky, particularly around the joints and behind my elbows and knees. Little bodily secretions come out when I scratch. I won't mention my cock; it's not pretty. And what interests me is not the ugliness. At least not of the cock. You can probably imagine or, if you have one, try the experiment for yourself. We'll see what happens after a week or two of normal climatic conditions; it's not nice to look at; no, you wouldn't slip this cock in your mouth.

It's a question of priorities; sometimes I like to feel dirty; it goes for the soul as well as the body. At some moments I like them to be greasy, and others dry and polished like the pieces of glass you pick up on the seashore. I imagine little hands caressing me. They'll put me at the bottom of a jar or an aquarium with lots of other bits of inoffensive glass, which, like me, will not cut any more but will decorate some bathroom or bedroom in a rented house, and now stationary, end their long maritime epic.

I'm rambling a bit. It's time to take a break, have a cigarette.

It's good stuff, this tobacco that burns your throat. And the paper that burns slowly. It can't be said often enough, the paper makes all the difference. I prefer it white and thick like drawing paper. The other stuff, the transparent type, goes out. And as a result a cigarette loses one of its most precious qualities, it ceases to be the moment, the moment which one devotes to smoking it, this metaphorical, I'd even say poetic, reminder of the passage of time, of life flowing away – whether you drag on it or not

– until death burns your fingers, burns your lips. I love that way of sending life up in blue smoke, like in the cinema, which seems to rise from the cigarette's tip to the ceiling.

My beloved cigarettes, which are criticised more and more.

The smoke that brings us closer to the heavens, to death; and the pleasure of the taste, the act of smoking, unequalled.

People are accused of starting smoking as an affectation of style. 'The style is the man': the saying is so well known, it's a bit shocking to quote it; schoolboy essay.

I accord a lot of importance to ashtrays. I hate putting my butts in glasses, or beer cans and bottles. I like stubbing them out, not in bottle tops or any old piece of stone, but in an ashtray that I've carefully selected. It's about the whole nature of the contact I have with these objects. I feel the material through the fag end; I caress them a bit when, as I press with the end of my index finger, making it turn firmly, I extinguish the ashy stub, the last piece of burning tobacco.

Of all the ashtrays I own, my favourite is the one I call the little gold one. It's round and palm-sized, and looks like it was made to rest in the palm of your hand. It's golden, a bit dented; it must often have been bashed on the floor, on walls and faces. It feels as though it's been through a lot, a terrible daily history of arguments and domestic dramas. It's old and time-blackened in places, particularly on the back of the little lid that snaps shut. That's what I like about it; when the lid is open it gives you somewhere to rest your burning cigarette, and when it's closed, it seals off its inner part, the container for ash and butts. When the cigarette is burning, it doesn't touch the container, doesn't set light to the ends in it and more important – and this means this ashtray, as far as I can remember, has always had a place by my bed – you can close the lid, which blocks the horrible smell of stale tobacco, that nasty smell that prickles your nostrils.

It's the only object I took when I fled; when I went to live with Emma.

I really loved her. She haunts me.

V

Armand is in the bar when Tobias rings.

'Hey, I'm glad you called. You OK?'

'Yeah, the hearing's over. They're sending me to detox. It can't be worse than prison. You know,

I tried to do myself in. With the Russians in my cell, we tore up the sheets to try and hang ourselves. But there was this screw who busted us. Funnily enough, I think that did me a favour. At the hearing, they said I was an addict; that I needed treatment. I'm going to be in detox for a month. I miss you, Loulou. You OK? You having fun?'

'Yeah, too much. I want to take a break.'

'Why?'

'Last Sunday when I got to the Pano, ten people said to me, "Shit, Armand, you were so funny last week, when you had your shirt off in the toilets and were jumping around". Shit, I don't remember a thing. I don't remember thirty-six hours of partying. That's fucked up.'

'But when I get out, you'll still come with me?'

'Yes, but I'll have to go easy. Look at the shit that it gets us into.'

'We're a good team all the same.'

'It's true, it's cool. Can't I come and see you?'

'I don't want you to see me like this. Anyway, I'll be out in a month.'

'Call me before then.'

'Have the others been asking about me?'

'Yeah, I told them you were in Paris.'

'Thanks, Loulou. OK, I have to go. Hugs.'

Armand hangs up. There's something touching about hearing a voice from so far away. Things are pretty fucked up for Tobias, Armand thinks, pretty fucked up for us both. And all for what? To dance together with your arms in the air. Yes, all this to raise your arms to the sky, feel a bit stronger and fuck in a toilet cubicle. For the first time, Armand sees the limits of this life. He's getting spots on the side of his face. It's not worth it if you do yourself so much harm, he thinks, just for a synthetic, manufactured pleasure. Tobias is in prison because he wanted to raise his arms to the sky, because he wanted to go on dancing for longer, and be stronger too. Too strong, too long. There's a sort of injustice to it. The unfortunate ones are punished because they don't know how to cope with their lives. The disorientated get downgraded. They rot like vermin, in little stinking cells, cells with rapists and snitches; they get treated like those bastards, the conspirators, the wicked. But they're not like them at all, they're not bad guys; they just wanted a bit of affection, a place in the world, an armchair or just a bench, a flip-down seat where they can sit with a bit of dignity. If all the useless people, all the losers and the parasites formed an army… if they formed an army, that would make some noise. More than people might think. They'd travel through towns and country; they'd march tirelessly to conquer a new order. A limping army, a bit fucked up, all the losers on the planet in a single regiment. Rogues, fuck-ups, artists and waitresses, tramps, the disinherited, cleaning women, night porters, party animals, plumbers and pen-pushers, all walking in sync, to create the place for themselves that they've never been given. They'd advance, with their improvised weapons, scaffolding tubes, bamboo poles and pepper sprays. Hide! They're coming; the forgotten people are rebelling. Postal workers, long-term unemployed, road sweepers, they're advancing towards this unnamable power, the power that imprisons lads like Tobias. They don't know where to strike; they'll burn everything. The humiliation has gone on too long. From the embers they'll build something new. They're angry, they'll burn everything. Piles of ashes, piles of ashes where they can sit down. Armand thinks about it. He smiles and cries. He goes home.

VI

Astrid has gone to work. Franz is bored. He could go gambling; he got the dole yesterday. But for the first time in ages, he's afraid. If he lost, what would he tell her? Astrid, baby, I've lost it all, not another penny will come in for a month. You're going to have to pay for my fags and grub, the electricity and the extras.

He knows she'd do it. But he can't, he can't ask that of her. Little Astrid, so sweet and pretty; she'll be cutting hair just now, telling her colleagues that she's met someone, a guy who's a bit lost, but he makes her laugh, it's so good to rest in his strong arms.

No, he can't do that to her. He would be too afraid of losing her too. Those few days spent with her were so nice, yet so simple, the joy of no longer feeling alone in this world.

She's a nice girl he can rely on. Best not disappoint her. He won't go gambling. He'll take a walk; no, he'll read, it's been ages since he did that.

VII

The walls here are a bit whiter, less grimy, more clinical. The screws wear immaculate overalls, but they aren't any less violent, no less inclined towards humiliation. As in prison, he's entitled to two walks in the park, one at 11 o'clock, the other at four; the timetable's equally strict: wake up at six, lights out at nine. The food is just as crappy, the people you share it with in the canteen, the other inmates, are no more reassuring than the cons. Here, just like in prison, he sees a psychiatrist every other day, they give him capsules to help him sleep, others to get him to wake up.

There is a difference, though; here Tobias is regarded as a patient and not as an offender. When he thinks about it, maybe a horrible illness *has* dogged him since adolescence (apart from the bad flu)? Maybe that's his problem?

PART FIVE

Spring

I

Little by little, the days are beginning to return to normal. The snows have melted, the pavements are clear. The sun reveals itself proudly, returned from who knows where, the antechamber of hell into which it had sunk. The trees on the boulevards strike poses, without trembling, growing new flowers, new leaves. People are back on their bikes, or just walking around, bareheaded, and sitting on café terraces again. It's as though there's a song in the air, something to hum as you watch other people going about their lives. Neurasthenics forget the misery of their condition for a while, as we all do; they go out and cautiously drink in the air. The mild weather takes hold of the body; it blows on the back of your neck like the wind of freedom. It's good to feel no longer spat out by the world.

These first days of spring, like a gentle revolution, overturn the established order. You have to make the most of it; it's worth it for the warmth.

II

Armand has done some shopping. This weekend he's going out, right to the end, from Thursday night till Monday morning. He feels a bit guilty, but he knows that sometimes it does you good to do yourself harm. Last weekend was the first time he hadn't gone out since he arrived. The first time too that he hadn't taken drugs. The only time in eight months. All the same, when you think about it…

Yes, but tonight will be great; they'll all be there, they'll recognise him. He'll dance, outside time, in the unreal world of the *druffis*.

Armand arrives at the Golden Gate. The bouncer shakes his hand; it's like they know each other well now; sometimes they get high together.

He goes in; plunging into the crowd intoxicates him. He rediscovers the pleasures of getting high together; all the regulars greet him and offer him some gear in the toilets. He dances until he can dance no longer, fucks in the cubicles full of filth. He takes his pleasure and gets wasted. A warm smile returns to his face. It all feels new to him, as though at last he has started living again.

He gets more and more wasted, until he forgets his body. He dances. He just dances.

Armand leaves the Golden Gate, his eyes wide open, as though he were waking up from a dream.

Tobias is coming towards him, carrying a rucksack.

'I knew you'd be here.'

'Oh, I'm really predictable.'

'I just got out. It's good to see you, Loulou.'

'You too. You OK?'

'I dunno. I feel funny.'

'Come on, let's walk.'

'Talk to me about something else. Tell me what you're doing. You painting at the moment?'

'Yes, I've been in a good phase for a few weeks. I think I've understood something. You see, I've never liked my generation. Facebook, texts, all that – it has no romanticism. And then, when I came here, and discovered techno and that whole scene, I felt like I belonged to my generation. And I think you have to be modern, absolutely modern. So, as I'm proud of my generation, I decided to stop running away from modernity. I want to abandon myself to it. I want to abandon myself to modernity. I can't remember who said this but it's something like: whoever puts his hand in the wheel of time gets his arm ripped off. I belong to my time; we have our music and our drugs. And I don't want to be like all the people who talk about that, but I have no choice; it's what I know, I have to paint what I know. So you have to try to not make too much shit, try to find a little poetry in all this fucking mess. Because I'm the product of my time. But I like old stuff; I never read living guys, they don't inspire my confidence. But at least as far as what I'm going to try to create is concerned, I need to forbid myself fleeing modernity. I need to attack it. It's not easy because it's crummy. But I have to go for it, there's no choice. You know, when Proust talks about the telephone, it's really great. I need to completely rethink my painting. I have to be of my time, because we *are* of our time. It's as simple as that, but I hadn't understood it. And that's something that has changed in me. I am abandoning myself to modernity; I'm stopping trying to flee it. Because we've certainly had some experiences; so there are things to say. Come on, let's walk a bit more. You want to come back to my place?'

III

From Armand's notebook:

Since last night, Tobias has been back on speed, GHB and ketamine. He seems happy enough about it (after being locked up); in a way, I can understand it.

On Thursday, when he got out, he was already thinking of Sunday's after. It's his life, I mean that that's the life he's mastered, there is no other. He says he's 'keen to see normal people', meaning the druffis. *He lacks the distance I still have, which enables me to say that it's not actually 'normal'.*

It's cold but I'm going to stay on the terrace; I need the air. The girls on Kastanienallee are blonde.

Feelings of guilt when I don't paint; hangover from my uni prep classes?

In any case, there aren't many days when I don't paint (at all). Maybe it's bad, maybe it's because I don't try hard enough to say the essential. I fill up white canvases but I don't say anything. I would prefer to fight against a lack of inspiration and when I paint only paint the essential.

This great loneliness (mixed with a breath of freedom) when you have no attachment.

Could I return to a normal life?

On the terrace, an old man on his own is leafing through a book; on the spine I make out: Alone in Berlin.

Only obstacle to a wandering life: the weight of books.

That obese workman working and sweating.

In the course of this notebook, the further I go, the more I retract. An echo of my life.

Study of personalities according to the drugs that suit them (and also cities).

What would I do with my days if I didn't read? Drugs for sure.

What I like about cigarettes is the satisfaction of taking a break (the pose too). You feel pride, with a fag in your mouth, you wait, you smoke.

I have more and more contempt for idleness. The idle irritate me. I like the tortured; the depressive exasperate me. Egocentrism of the depressive; in which there is nothing of the tortured.

The waiter's pride as a necessary bulwark against the humiliating aspect of his profession.

Ladies' men; dog men.

German women with a certain radiance, loving, a young child on the back of their bike.

The satisfaction of the busy cf. Proust p.1534: 'and also because of the satisfaction which the busy have – even if their work is the most foolish – of "not having the time" to do what you are doing'.

IV

This evening, Tobias and Armand are dining at Franz's place. The apartment has been cleaner since Astrid moved in; there are women's things here and there, like discreet decorations. A dress, a pair of boots left on the floor make the air in the living room seem purer somehow; they know that Franz is no longer alone, he has her by his side – a dress, a pair of boots left on the floor like witnesses to his happiness, his peace.

The dinner is nice. They do drugs without making a big deal of it. They talk about fresh starts. Tobias has brought his bag; tomorrow morning at six he's catching a train to Cologne. A job and an apartment await him there; a social worker will look after him, she has it all set up. This is their last evening together, Tobias is leaving Berlin and its parties. He looks delighted; he talks about it like a rebirth, finding himself again, far from the worries of the neon lights and the glitter balls. This time I'm really quitting, he says. Tonight is my last. I want to stay with you a bit longer, till it's time for my train. Then I'm starting a new life. I'll write to you.

Astrid, Franz and Armand aren't quite sure what they are experiencing, the gentle sadness of seeing a friend leave for a better life.

They talk about their memories, the adventures of the life they've shared. The time Franz's place flooded when they got back from a night out, the pipes that exploded without them realising because they were too far gone. The floor still bears the scars. And the time Armand collapsed from exhaustion on the dance floor at the Panorama. They talk about it with affection and nostalgia, as though they've returned from a long journey.

This evening Bar 25 is reopening. A last party and then Tobias will catch the 6 a.m. train to Cologne.

Bar 25

It's an outdoor venue, so this place is closed in winter. It's an open-air club on the banks of the Spree. Two bars on each side, like little bungalows, a swing attached to the branches of an old tree. People wander about, talking, like at a little funfair for adults. There are confessionals where people do drugs; a roof too, which shelters the DJ and the dance floor. There's a strange wind of freedom blowing here, everyone doing what they feel like; like a little park where the *druffis* all play together. There's a feeling of celebration, there's confetti, a crowded dance floor, the best

DJs of the moment, and all these places to walk about and dance. The celebrations here last all weekend, sometimes longer, until Tuesday. There are lockers to leave your stuff in. The more seasoned bring a toothbrush and deodorant with them, for this little trip that lasts several days. Everyone's happy to be here, it's an atmosphere that grabs you; you smile and dance. A play park for getting high.

Armand, Franz, Astrid and Tobias are dancing. They get high; it's the usual thing.

At 4 a.m. Franz and Astrid leave. They kiss Tobias and make him promise to write.

At 5.30 Tobias decides he'll catch the 9 o'clock train. He and Armand dance on.

At 9 o'clock Tobias postpones it a bit more; there's a train at 11, he'll get that.

Armand can't reason with him. At noon, he leaves; Tobias is still there, dancing, glitter dust on his face.

They won't see each other again. Armand won't allow himself to go that far. In the S-Bahn in the direction of the airport he gets caught by a ticket inspector for the first time in a year.

His grey notebook reads:

Work, pay fines, then die, to see what that's like.

That whole thing's dumb all the same. To want to escape from yourself.

'After a while it gets so bad that you want to stop the whole business.'